For Dotty (as ever)

Originally a teacher – because he loved the smell of plasticine – Keith Baty has spent most of his career in education bringing words and music alive for others. He lives on the beautiful Solway Coast, where the ever-changing sky helps him to create the landscapes that he puts into his novels.

**Keith Baty**

---

# ERIC BELL

AUSTIN MACAULEY PUBLISHERS™

LONDON * CAMBRIDGE * NEW YORK * SHARJAH

A CIP catalogue record for this title is available from the British Library.

ISBN 9781398479852 (Paperback)
ISBN 9781398479876 (ePub e-book)
ISBN 9781398479869 (Audiobook)

www.austinmacauley.co.uk

First Published 2024
Austin Macauley Publishers Ltd®
1 Canada Square
Canary Wharf
London
E14 5AA

# 1

When Terry Ellis told his mother he'd seen Eric Bell in Botchergate, she was sceptical.

"I didn't know you knew Eric," she said.

"He was a guard on the railway, wasn't he?" said Terry. "Before they turned into Train Managers."

She nodded and that was his cue to repeat the story of how, on the many occasions when Terry was the only passenger on the 0746 out to the coast, Eric refused to let him buy a ticket.

"One fare won't save this service," Eric had said.

Terry's mother seemed distracted. He pressed on regardless.

"Then there was that day when he pulled back his jacket and those watches were pinned inside. Just like an old-school spiv. At least he wasn't upset when I didn't buy one. Nor did he make me start paying for the train."

His mother looked at him.

"Eric?" she said. "Big Eric? Lived at the top of the road? When did you see him?"

"Yesterday," said Terry. "In that fog. But it was definitely Eric."

"Eric's been dead eighteen months," said his mother. "Now, can you put a new bulb in on the stairs?"

After fixing the light and pulling the bins onto the pavement, Terry walked up to the cemetery. At the main gates was the office of the Bereavements Manager.

"Is Ken McKie available please?" he said to the woman addressing envelopes in the cramped front office.

"Ken's up at an interment at the moment," she said. "Can I help?"

"Is there a map of who's buried where?"

"Just a minute," she said, and swivelled her chair round to the computer. "Who are you looking for?"

"An Eric Bell," Terry said. "Died about eighteen months ago."

She tapped on the keyboard. The screen lit up, but Terry couldn't see what was on it.

"There's three Eric Bells dotted about here. Let's see… May 23$^{rd}$ last year. That must be the one. He's up at the top end, adjacent to the toilets."

She smiled sympathetically at Terry. He didn't speak and she took this for delayed shock.

"Were you close?" she said.

"I hadn't…haven't seen him for thirty years. I moved away."

"I knew a June Bell and her father was called Eric. Big man. Worked on the railways."

Terry turned to leave.

"Thanks," he mumbled.

"He gave me a watch once," she said. "It never kept the right time."

Terry closed the door behind him.

**2**

The following day was November 5th. Terry's wife, Pat, was taking her Guides to the big bonfire in the park. For the second year in a row, Terry went along to look after Julie Diggle. Julie was, in Terry's view, a fantastic kid, so why did she have to have a life-limiting illness?

The year before, Julie had been able to walk with the aid of a stick. When Terry had last seen her, at the Summer Fete, she'd been on two sticks. Now she was in a wheelchair. Terry wanted to do more for Julie but, when he mentioned this to Pat, she said it wasn't appropriate.

"Her dad's gone off with a barmaid and her mother is in denial. She can barely cope but won't let anyone else help with Julie. She blames herself for the girl's illness. It runs in the family. She could have had a test but didn't."

"She'd have got rid of the unborn Julie?" said Terry.

"Who knows?" said Pat. "She took a chance and it didn't come off."

"She's had ten years. They've both had ten years. In that sense, it did come off."

At the end of the bonfire, Terry was pushing Julie back to the bus. The girl was giggling with excitement.

"I loved the giant Catherine Wheels," she said. "What was your favourite firework?"

"I was hoping there'd be Jumping Jacks," said Terry. "You don't see them now but, when I was about your age, my dad let one off and it jumped into the box where the other fireworks were kept. It set them all off as well."

Julie was still laughing as the ramp lifted her up into the back of the bus.

"Thanks," she said then the door closed.

Terry waved at her happy face as the bus drove off into the night.

Terry went back to the cemetery that weekend to look for Eric Bell. He walked up and down the muddy paths between the rows of gravestones but couldn't locate him.

*I should have asked the woman in the office for a map*, he thought.

He sat on a rusting metal bench outside the toilet block and gazed out across the winter landscape. In the distance, beyond the black metal railings and brown river, he saw the lights of the train coming in from the coast. He wondered if the guard – or Train Manager – was trying to sell jewellery of dubious provenance to today's customers.

After five minutes, Terry stood up and stretched, yawning at the late morning sky. As he brought his head down, he spotted Eric Bell's name. It was on a black marble gravestone. The stones on either side had mistakes on them. One said,

**IN MEMORY OF JOHN (JOHNNY) GREEN – LOVING HUSBAND AND BOTHER**

The other said,

**IN LOVING MEMORY OF MARY ELLEN. GONE TO HAEVEN**

In his mind's eye, Terry saw Haeven as a quiet coastal resort in Southern Europe. At this very moment, Mary Ellen was lying on a winter beach sunning herself, unaware that her holiday was being commemorated in a most unusual way.

*Eric wasn't there when I looked before but now, he is*, thought Terry. *It's like death in reverse.*

**3**

"I have to stop thinking," thought Terry. "But I can only do that by thinking myself into a state of not thinking. Is that possible? Perhaps Pat can help. Where is she?"

He looked at his hands, quivering by his sides. He was lying down. No, he was in bed. His was the only bed in the room. He could see a woman with a tea trolley.

"Tea?" she asked, smiling.

"Is there coffee?" he asked.

"There is. Sugar? Milk?"

"A little of each," said Terry.

He suddenly felt hungry.

"Have you a biscuit please?" he said.

"Yes," she said, depositing his drink and two Ginger Nuts on the bedside table.

As she wheeled the trolley out of the room, Terry caught a quick view of two people in the corridor. One looked like Pat. She was talking to a man with a beard. Terry didn't trust anyone with a beard: they always had something to hide.

Terry's friend Leo had a beard. At work, Leo couldn't walk along the corridor from his office to the stairs leading outside because it meant passing George's room.

It was all George's fault, but George wasn't to blame.

Leo found George impossibly attractive. Even glimpsing him brought Leo out in a kind of adolescent fever. Both men were married to women. Both couples had three children. George's wife was a sugar-rush: her presence instantly energised you. Leo's wife was a neutral on the energiser-to-drainer scale.

Leo wrote poems but hadn't shown them to his wife in years. Not since the day she'd told him that, because she was the one who always got up when the children cried in the middle of the night, her faculty for literary criticism was currently not even on the backburner. In fact, she'd laboured, it was right off the cooker and out of the kitchen.

He hadn't quite grasped the image but felt the sting of her disinterest to this day.

As he once again walked the longer three-sides-of-a-square corridor route to the stairs, Leo wondered if George liked poetry. He wondered if George loved his wife, the sugar-rush. He never wondered if his own wife had a point about his unwillingness to deal with crying babies. Or whether his poetry was any good. Mentally swatting away inconvenient questions was the superpower of the invincible narcissist.

Leo was, to borrow the phrase, 'a man who combs his hair in public.'

Despite being bald.

Terry was home from hospital. It was John (Johnny)'s widow who had come across him, sprawled on the tarmac 'twixt graves and public conveniences. Years earlier, she'd been a chief inspector in the police so had known where to look for identification and who to call for help.

Today, she'd come to visit him at his house. Terry didn't yet know about her career as a detective when Pat showed her into the living-room.

"There he is," said Pat. "I'll make us a drink. This is Mrs Green, Terry. She saved your life."

"Teresa," said Mrs Green as Pat left them together.

"It's a wonderful world," said Terry.

He was about to burst into song, but she was there first.

"I see Teresa Green, red roses too…"

Terry laughed stupidly, thinking of how Leo would have reacted to having the wind taken out of his sails like this. He wouldn't have liked it. Leo was a smartarse. Or is it smart arse? Two words. Is there a hyphen? Terry loved Leo as a brother but, like a brother, was less sure of whether he *liked* him.

"Funnily enough, my Johnny used to call *me* Terry but everybody else calls me Teresa," said Mrs Green. "It was our special thing."

Terry saw the faraway look pass briefly across her face and was – for no obvious reason – reminded of Julie Diggle, waving as the bus drove away from the bonfire.

**4**

Eric Bell felt the thawing droplets of freezing fog zigger down his face. He looked at Ernie Fox, all bad wig, and unnatural dentures.

"Come into the back," said Ernie.

"Camilla mustn't see me."

"Then it's a good job she's not here," said Ernie.

"I had to chance it," said Eric. "Was fairly sure today was your day in."

"Eric, she knows. You know she knows. Now, come into the back."

Eric lowered himself carefully under the shop counter and followed Ernie through. The fumes from the paraffin heater transported him back to late childhood, when he'd first come here. Time had moved on as, in turn, Ernie's grandad then dad ran the shop, squeezed a living from it then expired, leaving it to the next in line. The current next in line was Ernie but his nephew Willy was snapping at his heels.

"It's colder than a witch's tit out there," said Eric, his voice punctuated by breathy gasps.

"Eh?" said Ernie.

"I…" began Eric but the bell on the shop door rang and Ernie went out to see who it was.

Eric sat down and looked at Ernie's wet, fingerless gloves steaming on top of the heater. The odour of paraffin always made him want to sleep. He had just let the top lids of his eyes droop when he heard raised voices from the front, followed by a loud thwack and the sound of the shop door opening and closing forcefully.

Ernie came back through, an old school rounders bat in one hand and a shiny flapping £10 note in the other. Eric looked at him and raised his eyebrows. Ernie grinned.

"Couple of toerags trying to sell me insurance. Twenty a week and they'd look after the shop. See no one put the window out. Or in."

Eric nodded at the tenner.

"I obviously declined their generous offer. This is the money the smaller one gave me to not break his fingers like I'd just done to his pal."

"They only see old people," said Eric. "They don't see our experience."

"You're right," said Ernie. "Now Eric, tell me why you're here when you've been dead for eighteen months."

# 5

Terry was talking to Leo on the phone, explaining what he'd just explained to Teresa Green.

"They're not sure yet but I think it could be catalepsy. You go rigid. Lose any sense of where you are. Silas Marner had it. The symptoms are similar."

"Did you feel it coming on?" said Leo.

"I don't remember but the doctor said I must have sensed I was having an attack and lowered myself to the ground. The unconscious mind preserving the about-to-fall-over body."

"I didn't know about any of this."

"Neither did I," said Terry. "It's never happened before. They said it could have been brought on by stress. The internet tells me it could also be the start of Parkinson's or I'm suffering withdrawal symptoms from cocaine."

"You must be worried," said Leo.

"Well," said Terry, "it's more I *should* be worried but, somehow, I'm not. The time for panic is when the pathology report comes back."

Terry had no intention of panicking, but he often said things to Leo that reflected Leo's likely mindset rather than his own. If Leo had unconsciously dropped out of his surroundings, he'd be in a 24/7 crapping-his-pants funk. Terry preferred his trousers (relatively) clean.

"How are you feeling right now?" said Leo.

"Pretty much OK," said Terry. "But never mind me. What about you? How's the crisis going?"

"Crisis?" said Leo.

"George," said Terry. "How's it going with George?"

Before moving back north, Terry had seen Leo almost every day. Now that they lived 100 miles apart, contact was increasingly rare, but they managed to meet up two or three times a year for a walk. It was on their most recent ramble that Leo had confided his latest revelation.

"I have to tell somebody," he said. "It's burning me up."

"Naomi?"

"You don't tell your *wife* things like this," said Leo.

"She might have guessed already."

"No," said Leo. "I've been acting perfectly normal."

"That's always a giveaway," said Terry, trying to lighten the mood. "Well, you'd better tell me then."

# 6

Eric watched Ernie pour the boiling water into the cafetiere. He retained the gnawing sense that cafetieres weren't for the likes of him. He was from the instant coffee generation.

Ernie, five years older, almost qualified for the Camp Coffee club, austerity-led connoisseurs of the chicory-heavy concoction used when real coffee was scarce. That dated him, thought Eric, not sure of whether 'him' was Ernie or himself. There'd been that racism row about the Camp Coffee label around the turn of the twentieth century: the Sikh servant depicted waiting on a kilted Scots soldier as he sips his brew. People had suddenly decided to be offended by a century-old image.

Eric often wondered about what he thought of as flip-over points like this. Could you pin down the last moment before something generally acceptable became generally unacceptable? Was it related to the ability and means to express your indignation? Eric avoided social media. It helped him remain dead but, equally importantly, saved him from getting het-up about events over which he had no control (and, usually, no real interest in).

"Did the gollies on the jam-jar offend you?" said Eric as Ernie handed him the stained, chipped mug.

"Of course," said Ernie. "Not because I'm black but because those guys were so cool: astronauts, musicians, sportsmen…but no shopkeeper. I felt demeaned."

"Then again," said Eric, "they gave you something to aspire to."

"Huh," said Ernie, his eyes flashing disgust as he sipped his drink.

"And anyway," said Eric, "I thought they *did* have a golly gangster."

**7**

"She was very nice," said Terry. "Used to be a detective chief inspector in the CID. You'd never think it."

"Why not?" said Pat. "Because she looks like a little old lady and little old ladies were born that way? Never had a life?"

Terry considered the questions. He often looked at older people when he was out in the town, trying to see them as they must have been when they were young and fresh. Some were faded, diminished, but others were vibrant, spirited. It had little to do with age.

"She's not much older than us," said Terry.

He paused.

"She thinks she remembers Eric Bell."

"The same Eric Bell?" said Pat. "It's a common enough name."

"No, I gave her the story about the watches and the train. 'If it's coming back to me, it'll hit me at three in the morning.' That's what she said. She's visiting us again, whatever. Wants to make sure I continue to improve."

Pat went upstairs to get changed and Terry made beans on toast. They ate it on their knees.

"What's on tonight?" said Terry.

"A couple of Rangers are coming in to talk to the girls about orienteering. We're hoping to set up an event in the park in the next few weeks."

"How's Julie?"

"No better and no worse. No worse is about the best she can hope for. But she's got guts and she's always smiling. I think she gives the rest of the girls a bit of perspective. It's just her mother. She needs to back off."

"Is she still turning up? I thought you told her she didn't have the child protection clearance thing."

"She paid for one herself. It's hard to turn her away. She just wants to look after her daughter, but she'll alienate her eventually. Assuming Julie lives that long, that is."

Pat went off to Guides and Terry washed up. Random thoughts of Julie and her mother transmogrified into thoughts about Nicholas, a boy in the year above Terry in secondary school. Nicholas carried no image in Terry's head: he would never be able to put together an identikit picture of him, yet he had been an intermittent abstract presence in Terry's life since the age of twelve.

### 13 (*His age when he died*)

The Head of Lower School made the initial announcement in the first full assembly after the summer holidays. Newly re-caged, most of the audience still clung to the illusory freedom of the previous two months. Mentally pacing their confinement, they sought a way out and Mr Nuttall dangled one before them.

"The school has acquired an outdoor studies centre in the North Lakes. A residential week has been planned for the first week in October. Only Lower School pupils can go…"

(GROANS. Still *pupils* then, not *students*…)

"…but there will be an opportunity for Middle School after Christmas. Your form tutors will give you full details. Places are extremely limited. If demand exceeds supply, we'll draw names out of a hat. Michael Crane, see me after assembly and you can forget about going right now!"

Two days later, there was a buzz in the yard that a woman had been seen leaving Mr Nuttall's office in tears, shouting.

"She's got a posh accent, but she still called Mr Nuttall a knob," said Louise Anderson.

"She's right," said Marian Anderson (no relation – and no relations, according to her boyfriend).

"It was Nicholas in the third year's mother," said Trevor Lawson. "Nuttall doesn't want him to go on that residential. Because of that thing he has…"

"Nuttall?" said Terry.

"Nicholas," said Trevor. "He's got that fragile thing. Has to take it easy. Is it his heart? Could be his heart."

Next day, the list was posted of those going on the residential. There were 25 places but only 22 names so Nicholas couldn't be dropped on random selection grounds. He was in and, unless you were one of those going, the residential was forgotten as the term gained traction.

The Monday assembly after the group's return was late starting as Mr Nuttall hadn't yet arrived. Rising noise levels fell when he finally made his appearance, ashen-faced and uncharacteristically cowed. The collective first impression was that he was ill.

Voice cracking, he told everyone how you couldn't let disability define your life. He told everyone that Nicholas had died striving to break through his medical limitations. He told everyone that, from that point on, they should remember that each day they had in the world was another one more than Nicholas would ever see…

Terry, 40 years later at the sink, sobbed.

# 8

"It's not a good idea Eric," said Ernie. "You say no one'll recognise you but you can never be sure. Why risk it?"

"I know it's not reasonable, but I can't rest," said Eric. "I see it in my nightmares, and it opens up and I fall in and it closes behind me. Maybe if I see the real, actual plot, the nightmares will stop."

The following afternoon, the two men made their way up the winding road to the top of the cemetery. Progress was slow due to the residue of the previous night's frost stubbornly clinging to the tarmac. A couple of dog-walkers stared at them as they gripped each other for mutual safety.

"What are they looking at?" said Eric.

"Possibly those ridiculous sunglasses of yours," said Ernie. "It's late November and the sky's as dark as my arse."

They reached the toilets just as a few flakes of snow tumbled through the chilly air.

"Go and stand beside it while I have a pee," said Eric. "My bladder and cold don't mix."

Ernie hadn't been here since the funeral and criss-crossed from one row of graves to another, trying to find the headstone. A small woman laying flowers watched him for a moment.

"Who you are looking for?" she said.

"Bell," said Ernie. "Eric Bell. He's round here somewhere."

"He's right beside you," she said, pointing to the plot to the left of where she'd put the flowers. Ernie thanked her and tried to adopt a respectful posture as he read the inscription.

ERIC BELL
BELOVED GRANDAD, DAD, AND HUSBAND

Time has taken you away too soon
We'll never forget you
Carol, Bobby, Ted, and June

"What a lovely message," said the woman. "Which one are you?"

Ernie looked at her and shrugged, not understanding.

"Ted or Bobby?" she said. "Though these days, you might be Carol or June for all I know."

"I'm…I was just a friend," said Ernie.

Seconds later, Eric, still flapping wet hands, squeezed into position beside Ernie, the pair unwilling to stand outside the narrow width of the plot. He took off his sunglasses and breathed in heavily. The woman, watching him, slowly backed away.

"Well, I'll say goodbye," she said.

"Bye love," said Ernie then, nudging the silent Eric, "Say goodbye to the lady, Eric."

# 9

That night, there was a band rehearsal at Martin the drummer's new house and Gary, the bass-player, had offered to give Terry a lift. The two of them sat in darkness in the passing place on the narrow country road and squinted at the map on the sat-nav. It hadn't updated since they'd left the motorway ten minutes earlier.

"No signal," said Gary. "We'll have to ring and ask him exactly where he lives."

Terry's fingers crawled over the phone's keypad, and he put it to his right ear for a moment before proffering it to Gary.

"No signal," said Gary again. "We can't be far away. Somebody in one of those might know."

He put the car into gear and headed slowly for the row of big houses, one of which had early Christmas lights pulsing across the front garden. From nowhere, a tall figure ran in front of the car, arms waving frantically.

"In there," shouted Martin, pointing towards a path beyond a pitch-black gateway.

After decanting their guitars and gear into a small utility room, Terry and Gary followed Martin on a tour of the huge, semi-dilapidated farmhouse set in apparently large but currently unseeable grounds. Opening a door in the main corridor, Martin invited the pair to look inside.

The wet walls seemed to be crumbling and the room contained only a pile of different-sized paper sacks and a range of builder's tools. A musty malignant smell hung in the damp air.

"This'll be the master bedroom when it's been sorted," said Martin with an uncertain pride. "But the walls all need re-plastering. A thousand pounds each as it's a listed building. Needs special lime treatment. But it'll be reet…"

Gary and Terry glanced at each other, then looked away quickly.

The rehearsal was short and unsatisfactory, prematurely curtailed by Martin's pronouncement that he and his wife hadn't seen each other all day and, anyway, he needed his tea.

"We'll be winging it at the party," said Terry as they waved at Martin and motored back into the night. "That practice was much too short. The drive out here took longer. He wasn't interested."

"I think he's worried," said Gary. "He knows he's bitten off more than he can chew with that house."

# 10

It was a week after they'd been to the grave before Eric and Ernie met up again. December had arrived with a wet sluggishness missing from the covers of Perry Como Christmas albums.

This time, Ernie drove out to the caravan site on the coast where Eric was hunkering down for the winter. He parked in the 'Visitor' area and walked past bleak rows of dark, uninhabited mobile homes to Eric's place. It looked as gloomy and lifeless as all the others, but Ernie tapped on the smooth metal door and heard a muffled movement inside. The handle angled, the door creaked, and a narrow cross-section of human face appeared in the small opening.

"Ernie," said Eric in a low, furtive voice. "I nearly shit myself. Is there anybody about?"

"The *Mary Celeste* was more populous," said Ernie. "Let me in."

The interior of the caravan had the same overpowering paraffin odour as the back of Ernie's shop. The small blue flame of the heater provided the only light, reducing the sparse furniture to wavering shadows.

"An improperly adjusted wick causes smoke and odour," said Ernie, ducking in through the doorway.

"What?" said Eric.

"Is your heater switched off at night?" said Ernie.

"Yes. And it's adjusted properly. I've just put it on. That's why there's a smell."

"Just checking," said Ernie. "I worry about you. Don't want you dying of carbon monoxide leakage. Can we have a light on?"

In what was clearly a well-practised ritual, Eric quickly pulled the excessively thick curtains together. His hand then went for the light-switch but froze and he poked his head outside to confirm the absence of any other interlopers. His anxieties satisfied, he flicked the switch down and a pale-yellow bulb reluctantly flickered to life, casting a watery glow as it warmed up.

Meanwhile, Ernie had pulled from his pocket a bundle of envelopes held together with an elastic band. He threw them on the small table.

"I used to play the rubber trumpet…" he began.

"In an elastic band," said Eric. "Did these all come in the past week?"

He rolled the band off the bundle, picked up the first envelope and read the front.

"'To The Occupier'. Wonder how many of those there are here."

After sifting his post, he had a heap of circulars, fliers, and other junk mail, and a second, much smaller pile consisting of four items of personal correspondence.

# 11

Meanwhile, back in town, Terry was cycling to the hospital. It was results day following his incident at the cemetery. The rhythm of the pedals formed a backbeat to his thoughts. He was contemplating how several medical people at the hospital already had the news he was going to receive. They would have a plan. When he arrived, they would connect *him* to the currently uninhabited news and plan.

In his mind's eye, a familiar aerial view of the street corner came into focus. From one direction, someone slowly tottered along on crutches. From the other, someone was running behind a large dog (unleaded – not on a lead). A collision was inevitable but, in all the times Terry had experienced this mental film show, it had always shut down before he saw the consequences. Was he the large dog (probable victor in the imminent crash) or the wobbly pedestrian (to be sent flying)?

He was shaken from his daydream by the blast of a horn behind him. Turning, he saw a bullet-headed man in a cumbersome 4×4 gesturing at him. The man's hand was sweeping from side to side, and he seemed to be shouting. Terry looked around. The traffic lights they were waiting at were still red and, Terry knew, two other sets still had to change before his went back to green. The horn sounded again. Terry turned again, looked at Bullet-Head and shrugged. The window went down and the driver half-leaned out.

"Get to the side you wanker," said the man.

"I'm in the cycle box. I'm turning right," said Terry.

"Get out of the middle of the road," said the man.

Terry ignored him and faced forward. The light turned green. Terry didn't move. The horn started again. Terry didn't move. The light went back to red. Bullet-Head was shouting. Terry jumped off his bike, walked over the crossing in front of the lights and remounted, pedalling up the road towards the hospital.

He wondered what in Bullet-Head's life had made him turn out like that. Him, and thousands of other angry people. And why he hadn't got out of his big, pointless car.

# 12

Two of the personal items in Eric's pile felt, looked like and, when opened, *were* early Christmas cards. Neither had his name on and both came from people he didn't know.

"Are these the tenants we've had in?" he asked Ernie, showing the envelopes.

"One is," said Ernie. "The other might be. I didn't meet the second lot. The estate agent took over the leasing."

Eric tore the cards in half and threw them into the bin bag hanging below the table.

The third envelope contained a short, handwritten note. It said,

*Dear Brenda,*

*Thought I'd drop you a quick 'thank you' for the birthday present. My specs are cleaner than they've ever been, and I can see everything.*

*Love,*
*Kath*
*xx*

*PS Come and visit as soon as you can!*

Eric looked puzzled. Ernie read the note and creased his brow. Eric put it back in the envelope and dropped it into the empty fruit bowl beside the television.

The last envelope also contained a note, printed this time. It was on a small sheet of white paper and only two words long:

Hello Eric?

"Oh shit," said Eric. "Somebody knows."

"Don't panic," said Ernie. "It's probably speculative. From the life insurance company most likely."

"What?" said Eric. "I'm missing, presumed dead. Why use my name? This isn't a piece of business stationery. Somebody knows."

"Eric," said Ernie, "these firms have a respectable public face, all clean and shiny, and a hidden dirty face where grubby tactics might yield results. They've nothing to lose by trying to smoke you out. And this letter could have been there six months. It's that long since I went to the house."

Eric examined the envelope for a clue, but the stamp hadn't been franked. He sat down on one of the low uncomfortable benches and began to tear at his hair, his breathing becoming heavy and uneven. Ernie squatted in front of him and looked into his friend's watery eyes.

"Come on Eric," he said, in what he hoped was a reassuring tone. "Think of Carol. Whatever happens next, it was worth it for Carol."

<h1 style="text-align:center">13</h1>

Terry, in the anteroom of the Neurology Department, was almost embarrassed to be there. The place was full, and he didn't feel unwell. Staff in a bewildering variety of uniforms, each designating some doubtless specific but, to him, unfathomable rank, or role, chased around between innumerable other rooms leading from this hub.

He took stock of his surroundings. His fellow customers covered a wide age spectrum, from two babies (one crying, the other uncannily silent) to several undeniably very old people. The majority appeared to be men and women of somewhere between 25 and 40, though Terry knew that appearances were often deceptive.

Everyone was white-skinned, if that was the currently acceptable descriptor for those with light pigmentation. Terry wasn't sure it was, but no alternatives came to mind. Ludicrous questions popped into his head following this observation: was this a whites-only clinic? Did having darker skin immunise you against neurological disorders? (He was sure this wasn't true.); was the NHS biased against non-whites?

He stopped himself mid-thought. This looping mental activity could, he knew from repeated experience, both exhaust and destabilise him. To calm down, he looked at the room itself. At one end was a token attempt at a small play area for children in the form of a school-size desk and two chairs. A box of brightly coloured plastic toys and 3D shapes sat on top of the desk and Terry speculated as to how many germs were living on the plastic.

The walls of the room were covered in a standard, neutral, magnolia emulsion, recently applied. He knew this, not only because the paint looked clean but because a big-faced clock had been propped on top of a radiator, having apparently dropped off the wall. The circle of space it had inhabited remained pale blue.

"Who paints a wall with a clock still hanging on it?" said Terry to the youth beside him looking at his mobile.

The youth ignored him, opiated by the small, coloured bricks Terry could see dancing across the phone's screen. From plastic to pixelated in 10 short years.

Terry's appointment was for 2.30 but everyone was running late, a fact emphasised by several loud and angry protestations made to the two receptionists. Terry didn't mind the delay, but the complainants annoyed him.

*They don't have to wait*, he thought. *They're free to go home.*

But, of course, they didn't.

At 3.35, his name was called, and he was directed into a room with

## P DALZELL

scrawled in purple ink on a wipe-clean notice screwed to the door. A middle-aged woman and a younger man sat adjacent to a large table mainly filled by a computer monitor, files, and small items of medical equipment. A female nurse in a dark blue uniform hovered off to the left, adjusting the curtains around an examination bed.

The middle-aged woman stood up and smiled. She looked completely exhausted.

"Penny Dalzell, consultant neurologist," she said, holding out her hand. Terry shook it and nodded at the man, who was still seated.

"I'm sorry for your wait," she continued. "We have a doctor off sick. Do you mind if my colleague listens in on our discussion? He has a special interest in this area?"

"Er…no," said Terry. "This area? What is 'this area'?"

"Please," said Penny Dalzell. "Take a seat."

# 14

It was dark when Ernie arrived back home. Only 4.00pm and the last patch of daylight had disappeared. He parked the car in the drive and walked quickly down to the town to close the shop. Their usual weekday woman was ill so Camilla, his wife, had been looking after it for the afternoon but he knew how much she hated dealing with customers.

He'd left Eric in an anxious state. He felt bad about it but also knew that anxiety was one of Eric's core characteristics. Eric would have to calm his own demons on this one.

The dustbins, emptied that morning, were still out in the back lane so Ernie pulled them into the yard and entered the shop through the rear door. As he did so, Camilla came through from the front. Her expression was enough.

"What's happened?" he said.

She was the last person he knew who could be intimidated so she just reported the facts.

"Some teenager with a bandaged hand. Came in and asked if the man who served in the shop was in any time. I said you'd probably be back at the end of the afternoon. He said he'd call again around five."

"It didn't occur to you to lie and say I *wouldn't* be back today?" said Ernie, grinning broadly.

"Would I ever lie for you, Ern?" said Camilla, grinning herself then, serious, "The boy looked…off. He had that look that you sometimes have. I figured you might as well get it all settled as soon as."

Ernie nodded and filled the kettle. He perched in front of the paraffin heater and waited. Camilla went back to the counter to close the till for the day. He never lost the feeling that he was extraordinarily privileged to have Camilla. She was his homing beacon when he traversed his various valleys of darkness. No one else mirrored his own fatalism so fully.

A few minutes later, he heard the shop door open and two people enter.

"Is he back yet? And don't try lying," said a young, excitable voice.

"Hey boy, don't be rude to the lady," said an older man.

"Someone to see you!" shouted Camilla.

Ernie got up and went through. The older man smiled.

"This him?" he said to the youth beside him.

"That's him, grandad. That's the psycho twat who bust my fingers. You've had it now, you old fucker."

Ernie looked at the two of them then nodded imperceptibly at Camilla, who discreetly withdrew into the back room.

"You broke two of my grandson's fingers?"

Ernie nodded.

"Trying the squeeze on you, was he?"

Ernie, impassive, nodded again. The man turned to face the youth.

"You wanted money to leave this man alone? This *old fucker*?"

The youth nodded enthusiastically, not reading the signs.

"And he broke your fingers and sent you and your mate running?"

The youth nodded again.

"And you want me to sort out your mess-up?"

The boy now looked less certain.

"You're the hardest man in this town, grandad, and he needs to know it."

The man looked at Ernie.

"Sorry about the boy, Ernie," he said. "He's a disgrace to my good name and I'm ashamed to stand beside him."

"But grandad…"

"Piss off home, boy. I'll see to you later."

Angry, confused, and reluctant, the youth slunk out into the early evening darkness. Ernie looked at the man.

"Brian," he said. "I thought you were living in Portugal. How long's it been?"

"Too long," said Brian. "So, what you doing running a shop?"

# 15

"They didn't find anything?" said Pat. "Will it happen again?"

Terry faced her across the kitchen table, their evening meals half-finished on the plates in front of them.

"I don't know," said Terry. "They don't know. It's one of those conditions with multiple possible causes. We identified a few it wasn't, like drugs, and they don't think it's Parkinson's or epilepsy. The MRI didn't show anything."

"So, what's next?"

"Nothing, for now. We wait and see if I have any more attacks like the cemetery. If I do, I've got a hotline to the doctor who's interested in cases like mine. But honestly, I feel fine. The same as I always have. Try not to worry and, if you do, hide it or you'll make *me* worry and *that* might set it off…"

His attempt to make light of it didn't work. She turned away from him and ran out of the room and upstairs. He heard her crying and went up to comfort her. She beat her fists against his chest until he took hold of her wrists and she fell limp against him.

"Sorry," she said. "This isn't like me, is it? It should be good that they didn't find anything."

"Let's go downstairs and I'll go through everything the consultant told me again."

He managed to calm her enough so she went to her weekly dance class. Left alone on the sofa, he pondered his situation. He wasn't particularly worried about the inconclusive diagnosis. What really concerned him was his mushrooming sense of disconnection from events around him.

Not too long ago, his earlier encounter at the traffic lights would have had his adrenaline levels up in the danger zone but today he had felt essentially nothing. It was becoming a disturbingly familiar experience, this non-reaction to life.

# 16

The English seaside on a Sunday afternoon in December is, like cough medicine, an acquired taste. Eric hadn't acquired it but recognised that, again like cough medicine, you sometimes just had to take it if you wanted to feel the benefits. His conversation with Ernie earlier that week had disturbed him for several reasons, the main one being the mention of Carol. He was now squatting in this mini-Brutalist bus shelter in pouring winter rain because of her.

As the wild grey sea lurched ever closer to the wall behind him, his gaze remained fixed on the supermarket over the road. Its glaring yellow lights were an incongruous addition to the windswept seafront, a melancholy reminder of the days when late-season holidaymakers filled this same space to gaze at the annual illuminations strung along the full length of the promenade.

Eric had been here two hours already. Unfamiliar with the supermarket's opening times, he'd over-erred on the side of caution and arrived much too early; but he didn't want to miss her.

At just after 4.30, the last customer had walked out of the shop, a stretching silhouette hurriedly disappearing into the darkness beyond. That was an hour ago and Eric was beginning to panic that Carol might have left by another door. Or not come to work at all today. He didn't – couldn't – go in to check earlier. That was absolutely off the cards…the table… Completely impossible.

Shuddering, he tightened his scarf and tried to block the elusive gap in the collar of his coat that was still letting the wind in. Then – there she was. He just had time to see that *her* coat was too short before the gloom consumed her. Eric stood up and, as he did so, felt his cold muscles resist his intention to move before he bullied them into motion and set off after his wife.

# 17

The same afternoon, back in Cumbria, Terry was physically and mentally wandering. It was a small city, easily walkable. These days, he knew it as a succession of amorphous places that he almost had pinned down to two main manifestations: the one where he spent his early years and this newer version, which had evolved in the years he and Pat had lived away. He was often reminded of his friend Neil's reply when asked to nominate his favourite place in the world.

"Silloth," he'd said decisively then, after a pause, "In the August of 1969."

Time was a tricky customer, a shapeshifter, an agent of uncertainty, an inconstant partner impossible to throw off. Time had the outward appearance of a line but the concealed innards of an uncuttable Gordian Knot.

Gordian Knot became Gordon Notman as Terry passed the football ground. Passed the football…go for it…missed the goal.

Terry's junior school used to pick the school team exclusively from the Year Six class. A tradition. Gave the boys – still just boys in a football team then – something to aspire to before they fragmented the following September:

"Put up with the basket-weaving and the sewing and the WOMEN, TOO MANY WOMEN, for three years and your reward shall be cold afternoons outside in thin soccer strips. This will make MEN of you. A-Men."

Twelve boys in Terry's class and Terry, not interested and secure in his disinterest (though it's really 'uninterest' but that's not a recognised noun) was always the substitute. Number 12. Running the line to keep warm. Called on once in the whole season, scored an own goal and taken off. The team struggled to victory with just 10 men. MEN.

He was Number 12, but Gordon Notman was Number 9 and that was really Number One because the centre-forward was the spotlight position. The reserve of the best player. ('Isn't a reserve a kind of player too?' Find out below.) Adulation guaranteed. And Gordon Notman was not only the best player but, against all expectations, a humble boy. He had a quiet confidence and no inclination towards *braggadocio.* Capable in the classroom and a 'future prospect', as Mr Coulthard, Year Six teacher put it, on the soccer field.

His legendary dribbling made him a target for hard tackles in matches, but he seemed to float above efforts to stop his relentless pursuit of goals. At 14, he was picked out by the local Division Two club's scout, went for a trial and was signed up. Training weekly with a moderately successful professional team, he remained, despite the constant attention at school, decent and modest.

At 16, the week before his planned first game with the club's reserves, his overtired lorry-driving Dad didn't see him standing on their driveway and ran him over. A broken leg and vague 'internal injuries' were the report at school. His dad was inconsolable, possibly suicidal, they said. Gordon would never play again, went the rumour, and the worshippers looked for other gods.

Though not really more than an acquaintance, Terry went to visit him in hospital. Took him something to read. Took him, in fact, his cherished *Roy of the Rovers Summer Special,* the one where Roy Race has his ankle smashed in a car crash. Terry thought carefully about this: would Gordon find the story inspirational or unrealistically optimistic? Keeping the comic in a carrier bag beneath the hospital bed as he talked to Gordon, he didn't decide to hand it over until the last moment before he had to leave the ward.

When he went back for a promised second visit a week later, Gordon had gone. Moved to a bigger, specialist hospital on the other side of the country, according to the latest story. After a couple of months, Terry went to Gordon's house. Assuming the woman who answered the door to be Gordon's mother, he discovered that she was in fact the new owner.

"We've just moved in," she said. "The sale was very quick. The previous people wanted to move over the North-East."

Two years later, Terry of the sixth-form arrived home to find an unfamiliar car outside the house. Inside, Gordon Notman, his dad and Terry's dad were waiting. Gordon stood up and held out a magazine. *Roy of the Rovers.*

"You're the only one came to see me in hospital. It meant a lot. I'm sorry it took so long to get in touch, but we moved away. I wanted to give you this back. That story got me through some rough patches, but I made a full recovery. I'm on the books with…"

Terry, now, didn't reach the end of the long-ago sentence.

# 18

Eric felt like Cyril Jubb. Or aged 17 again, when he first met Carol at work then took to ambling past her house, not brave enough to go to the door and ask her out. Her father spotted him eventually and hauled him into the parlour (dating him, '*parlour*'), asking,

"What are your intentions towards my daughter?"

whilst holding a (replica, though Eric didn't know it then) shotgun. His stammering attempts at a reply hadn't impressed old man Brown but Carol, a witness to this threatened execution, was won over.

Now, at the other end of life, here was Eric once again staking out the only woman he'd ever loved, differently but equally unable to approach her.

Ernie wouldn't be happy if he could see him now, breaking his promise. But it was Ernie who'd unwittingly pointed him towards her after Eric's death.

"It's done. You're cremated, the house is on the market and she's back somewhere she knows. She's safe because no one wants to get her. They wanted you but you're gone."

As this was the only place Carol and he had ever lived outside of their hometown, 'somewhere she knows' hadn't been hard for Eric to identify.

He'd waited almost a year before deciding to try and find her. After many fruitless visits spent carefully wandering around the small resort, he'd begun to doubt that she was here after all. Then he'd almost blown down the whole house one day in early summer.

Worn out by another exhausting morning of covert searching, he'd let his concentration lapse. Stumbling up the concrete ramp to the railway platform, she'd disembarked right in front of him from the train he was here to catch. With only half-a-dozen other people around, Eric had no option but to bluff it out. Hide in plain sight!

He kept walking, passing less than an arm's length from her, sick with love and fear. Twisting his neck slightly, he was just able to glimpse the back of her head and take in the blue checked supermarket overall hanging below the bottom of her jacket.

Frightened by this near-miss, Eric avoided returning until the summer passed and the nights lengthened. At first, he'd only wanted to confirm she was really here. Now, knowing where she lived, his fear had changed shape. Now, he wished he'd kept his fortitude. Now, he would have a daily fight with the insistent temptation to travel down and just look at her.

He really should have listened to Ernie.

# 19

"Are you OK?"

Terry's hand was stiff. It seemed frozen to the incongruous bronze statue of the footballer silhouetted against the yellow streetlights. Gordon Notman was on the books with…who? He turned his head.

"Are you OK?" said the voice again. "Only, you've been there since we went out shopping and that was three hours ago."

The couple with the pram were looking at him anxiously. The woman held the pram handles, which were draped with loudly declared in blue and red letters, Bags For Life.

"If I ran a dating agency, I'd call it Bags For Life," said Terry, confused, trying to bring reality back into focus.

"What's that?" said the man. "Do you need an ambulance?"

"Ambulance…?"

Terry disengaged his hand and his arm flopped uselessly down, all feeling numbed by cold and pins and needles.

"What time is it?" he said.

"Just after seven," said the woman. "Mike, call an ambulance."

"No," said Terry, his arm slowly reviving. "Thank you but I'm alright now. I must…this happens sometimes."

"We live just there," said the man, indicating a high mid-terraced house on the other side of the road from the soccer ground. "Come and have a warm drink. It would make us all feel better."

The front room was cosy, and Terry sank gratefully into the deep cushions of the sofa. Closing his eyes, he heard a coffee machine and the low clatter of tins being put away. A baby cried briefly as footsteps faded up a creaking wooden staircase.

*Aunt Mimi had that creaking staircase in her Edinburgh town house. She'd put him in the basement and Claire in the attic bedroom the night they stopped off to see her on their Scottish AWOL trip. It took three hours for him to realise he'd never get up to reach Claire without disturbing Mimi. He could still recall the late-teenage frustration of those slow hours crawling towards dawn…*

*It was after that same trip that Claire, who'd told her father she was visiting her university roommate in Taunton, had asked him to pick up photos at Boots. Her father had handed her the packet with a smile, saying,*

*"It looks like Alison has changed sex and Glasgow city centre has moved to Somerset."*

*For the rest of their brief relationship, Claire's dad would always greet Terry with a wink and a,*

*"Hello Alison…"*

*Terry had really liked Claire's dad.*

Mike brought in the tray of coffee and biscuits and put it on the fireside table.

"Helen won't be long," he said. "She's just putting Lizzie to bed. If you need to call anyone, use my phone. I'll leave you to it for a minute."

# 20

Terry, in a strange house. Eric, outside one, two hours and two train lines away. Ernie, in familiar territory at home.

Camilla and he were finishing off their evening meal, she occasionally glancing at the small TV halfway up the kitchen wall, Ernie languidly turning pages of the newspaper beside his plate. Now and again, he would unconsciously tune into the televised version of the written facts before him.

The big story of today was the stalker, in prison at last, but still intimidating his celebrity prey with letters smuggled out and mysteriously posted.

"How can they not stop him writing to her?" said Camilla. "He harasses and follows her for four years before the police get him. Four years!? That poor woman. We only had the one do and that was bad enough."

Ernie grunted in what he hoped was a neutral tone. It was maybe 40 years since that 'one do' and he was happy to consign it to one of the many files marked 'Closed' within his memory. There was no need for Camilla to ever have the full details.

He had been working at the Grange then, managing the restaurant-cum-cabaret club. With her husband habitually out at night, Camilla began regular twice-weekly trips to the bingo with Barbara from next door. Most games were for prizes rather than money but there was a 'Windfall Night' on the last Saturday of the month, when *up to* £250 could be won in a single game.

The Rex, a cinema before television culled it, sat between the Co-op and an old-style hardware shop in the local shopping *street* (not *centre*). Bingo evenings began at 7.30, ended at 10.30, and there was a half-hour break around 8.45, distinguished by the thick cigarette smoke floating down the pavement as the women left their plastic tabletop boards and surged out for ironic fresh air. Men at a bingo game (callers excluded) were as rare as male infant teachers, two nearby pubs being provided for their social outletting.

Camilla and Barbara could never pin down when they were first aware of him, his presence a slowly lengthening shadow that eventually becomes obvious. It was a Wednesday evening in March when he introduced himself.

The walk from home to the club took them down a winding hill past a reclaimed council tip, a church and a park before the street levelled out and the shops appeared. Thinking back later, they both remembered regularly glimpsing the lone figure standing at the park gates between the cast of the streetlights and the darkness beyond. But it hadn't seemed significant enough to mention at the time.

*This* night, he stepped out in front of them, and they had no choice but to stop.

"'Scuse me, ladies," he said, and the two would recall how those three words alone had sent out some primeval alert. "I'm looking for a Hardy Street."

Clever to pick a destination that was further along their route to the bingo. No real option other than to invite him to walk alongside them.

"Thank you, girls," he said, leaving them (no longer ladies).

He was in the phone box opposite the Rex when they came out at the end of the session, staring at but not acknowledging them, no pretence of making a call. Neither Camilla nor Barbara said anything, but the walk home was brisker than usual.

The Saturday night, he was there again, leaning on one of the park gateposts.

"Well," he said as they approached. "You two again. Do you come here often?"

Laughing.

"Did you find who you were looking for?" said Barbara because something needed to be said.

"What?" he said.

"The other night. In Hardy Street."

"Oh yes. I found them alright. In fact, I'm going back there now. I'll walk with you."

"It's OK. We're in a hurry," said Camilla.

"I'm sure I can keep up with you two fit little beauties."

For the next four bingo nights he was in the same place, the ambiguous banter pushing the boundaries a little more each time. Nothing you could really put your finger on but they all three knew what was happening.

The day Barbara said she didn't want to go to the next session, Camilla told Ernie.

"She said he reminds her of Benny and it's taken her God knows how long to stop worrying about *him* coming back. This bloke just talks to us, but I think he's been watching us for a while. Barbara's scared he'll follow us home, find out where she lives. If he hasn't already."

"Tell her to stop worrying," said Ernie. "I'll sort it."

Ernie came up behind him at ten to seven the next Saturday. After playing look-out for ten minutes, he'd seen him arrive and take position inside the bushes at the park's main entrance. Ernie circled round and concealed himself in more bushes further down the path.

He watched the man nervously – or was it excitedly? – looking at his watch. There was a chance this wasn't the one who'd been intimidating his wife and her friend, but it was a chance Ernie had no qualms about taking.

Ernie clapped his hands and the man turned.

"Who…?" he said then he was on the ground, his legs knocked out from beneath him.

His cries grew weaker as Ernie systematically and silently disabled both arms then both feet with experienced blows from the steel-toed boots. It was over in seconds.

Ernie crouched down and helped the man to his feet.

"Take me to your house," he said, a final protest shortened by a tight jab to the right eye from Ernie's balled fist.

Half-staggering, the man led Ernie to an expensive semi on the new estate by the river. He stopped at the front door.

"Who are you? What do you want?"

"You've been following my women. Open the door."

"But I haven't done…"

Ernie hit him again and the man found his key and put it in the lock.

"My wife and kid are…"

Ernie kicked the door fiercely and it swung back against the table in the small hallway, sending a glass dish crashing to the floor. A blonde woman holding a blonder child's hand appeared at the top of the staircase.

"Tony?" said the woman. "What…"

"Goodnight Tony," said Ernie. "I'm trusting you to behave yourself from now on."

Ernie, today, said to Camilla, "Switch that telly off, love and let's go out for a bit of air."

# 21

Eric was running back along the promenade, icy rain peppering him as he headed for the last train of the night. In his right ear, the lurching tide was now sweeping in without inhibition, roaring like an extremist. To his left, the heavy hailstones battered against the windows and wooden shutters of businesses closed for the winter. Litter, liberated from runaway wheelie bins, spiralled wildly across the road and into the sea.

The train was just pulling away when he jumped onto the platform. As the handle of the rear carriage slipped from his grasp, his desperate eyes met those of the guard (*Train Manager?*) behind the locked door. Eric, heaving with exhaustion and shivering with cold, watched the red rear light receding into the black night then stop and begin to crawl back towards him.

"God, thank you," he said breathlessly, as the guard helped him in through the newly released door.

"It's against the rules but I couldn't leave you out there on a night like this. I'd rather you didn't tell anybody."

"I used to do your job," said Eric. "There was a lot of balancing the rules against customer needs. I appreciate it."

He went to sit down, the only passenger in the two coaches. The guard strolled down the aisle and Eric pulled out his rail pass.

"Don't worry about that," she said, taking the seat opposite him. "How long were you on the railway?"

"Thirty years," he said, adding, "Some of them on this service."

"It's a funny time to take a trip down memory lane," she said.

"If only you knew."

Thirty minutes later, he'd long left the rundown branch unit on the buffers in the connecting station and was hurtling northwards along the main line through the Lakes.

It was almost midnight when he arrived back at the caravan park. The chilling ride out from town had been punctuated by careful traverses through the various floods that had accumulated on the road. He had managed to get through before the same tide that had lashed him on the promenade earlier had surged this far north and cut off the road completely. Locking the scooter away, he was glad he lived here and not in the village a mile further on. There, the storm would have no mercy.

Waiting for the kettle to boil, he thought again of Carol. She was at least living in a decent place at the better end of the prom, though he hadn't been able to work out if she occupied the whole house or just a part of it. The building had been in darkness when she'd arrived home, so it seemed unlikely that anyone else shared it.

And what if they did?

He had no further claims on her, no control over her actions. She was his widow, had been for almost two years (if you included the four months when he was merely missing, not yet presumed drowned). She had a right, if not a duty, to move on with her life. And at this thought, he once again panicked.

What if she *had* met someone else?

He filled the hot water bottle and took it into the bedroom. The rain on the roof was louder than in the lounge and he wasn't optimistic about getting an undisturbed night's sleep. He was too agitated by the day's events anyway. As he slipped the bottle between mattress and duvet, he reached for the drawer in the base of the bed. From it, he took out the large black scrapbook. He knew it was futile to relive it all again, but he couldn't help himself. Pulling back the front cover, he began to read.

# 22

Pat collected Terry despite his protestations. He wanted to walk but could tell she was worried when he rang so acquiesced. She thanked Mike and Helen for their kindness, and they confirmed what Terry had told her.

"Do I take you home or do we stop off at Accident and Emergency?" she said in the car.

"I haven't had an accident and I feel fine," he said. "What could they do for me tonight? It's still the weekend and they'll be swamped with drunks and druggies."

Terry, reheated and back in his own living-room, felt better than fine. In truth, he hadn't felt unwell at any point during either of his two incidents: he had just ceased to be for a short while.

Later, when Pat went to bed, he put on some music and tried to figure out what was happening to him. He found it hard to get any further than,

*"My brain seems to speed up then, when it can't take any more, stops to recover."*

Except, in the mix, there was something about the past. It was like a slumbering force, awakening to invade and disrupt the present.

Never a sentimentalist, Terry couldn't understand why long-dormant incidents erupted more and more often, and with a power he could neither foresee nor control. When it happened, he wasn't just remembering he was there, watching things unfold again. Deja vu? Parallel universes? Developing schizophrenia? The last option would fit in with the catalepsy, as he still labelled it.

He was deep in such thoughts when the phone rang, unusual for this late on a Sunday (or any other) night.

"Hello?"

"Terry? It's Naomi. Leo's had it."

"Had it? What do you mean?"

"He didn't recover."

Terry was silent, unable to think of what to say.

"From the attack," she continued. "It finished him off."

His oldest friend's wife began to cry tinnily in his ear. Terry looked dumbly at the receiver in his hand. What attack?

# 23

# Woman Dies in Fall from Train

The first paper was splitting in places at the edges of the pages. There were yellowing streaks and little tears (*tears: rips, not eyefalls*) along the creases. A line of ink trapped within a fold had almost disappeared. Eric smoothed the paper out carefully. The sense of helplessness revisited him. He had no power to change the 25-year-old report, despite its terrible inaccuracies.

Pre-Internet, it remained, the contemporary record of what had happened at the time. *(Is the second comma necessary in the previous sentence?)*

Pre-Internet, it remained the contemporary record of what had happened at the time. *(It is.)*

Eric, starting a quarter of a century ago, had mentally consolidated a faithful recall of the sequence of events leading to the tragedy. *This* report and its follow-ups had provided a constant, obsessive inspiration to develop an objective overview of a clearer truth.

**WOMAN DIES IN FALL FROM TRAIN**

That day…

Working another early shift on the coastal route, Eric had already been out and back once, the train inhaling and exhaling customers in line (ha!) with how closely arrival and departure times matched school, factory, and business hours along the route. The next run mopped up and deposited the second wave of workers at the first three stops, usually leaving the carriages empty until the next big town was reached and the daily shoppers began to appear.

On the day it happened, a man and woman got on at the departure station and soon became the only passengers. Eric, ordinarily quite happy to sprawl in his little cab at the rear of the train, was somehow unable to relax. The two were sitting at the top end of the front carriage, just behind the driver, but Eric could nevertheless hear them arguing. Or, at least, could hear him shouting at her.

At the next station, despite it being a request stop and no one making a request, Eric buzzed to halt the train. He jumped down and walked up the platform, trying to spot the couple. He knocked on the driver's window.

"Everything OK, Eric?" said his colleague in muffled tones. "Only, we're a bit behind time already…"

"Can you hear him ranting at her?"

Eric's face was pressed against the glass, flattening his nose.

"Can't hear anything in here. Insulated against the outside world. Bliss! Shall we go?"

Eric tried again to see the pair as he strolled back down the platform. They weren't in their seats and the carriage was empty. He slowed down as he passed the middle door. Through the scuffed window, he glimpsed them standing in the vestibule, the man gripping the woman's right arm. Uneasy, Eric reached his cabin, buzzed again and the train rattled into motion.

Now he was leaning forward on his seat, the cabin connecting door open, trying to hear what the still-shouting man was saying. When he heard the smack and the scream, it was time to step in. He stood up but was thrown backwards as, without warning, the train shuddered to a stop.

## WOMAN DIES IN FALL FROM TRAIN

There is only one high point on the coastal route, when the line crosses a deep valley with a river running through it. It was here, at the centre of the Victorian viaduct, where the train was now stranded, the open carriage door swinging out across the edge of the bridge.

Eric, back on his feet, rushed up the aisle between the seats. Inside the driver's cab, he knew his colleague would be informing the control office of the current situation. It was standard practice in case signals had to be changed immediately. Finding out why the communication cord had been pulled was Eric's job.

The male passenger was looking down to the valley bottom, one hand on the door handle to steady himself. There were still manual doors and windows then: anybody could open them and sometimes they opened accidentally. Yesterday's mistakes inform today's improvements.

"She just slipped, and the lock gave way. She fell out. I pulled the cord to stop the train."

The man displayed no emotion as he related this and Eric didn't believe him. Later, at the inquest, the man would say it was shock that explained his lack of feeling but Eric had been there on the day. He'd looked into the man's vacant eyes and thought,

"He killed her. Humour him."

It wasn't an unreasonable position to take.

Over 45 minutes passed before the police – transport and local – arrived at the far end of the viaduct. With no footpath alongside the line, there was no alternative but to run the train off the bridge onto solid ground. The man was taken away for questioning. The driver and Eric were questioned, asked to make statements then sent home. The train, in readiness for forensic investigation, was steered to the nearest siding by a different driver.

## WOMAN DIES IN FALL FROM TRAIN

Eric looked at the headline again, carefully refolded the newspaper and, placing it on the bedside cupboard, picked up the second instalment of his self-curated collection.

"That would have confused me as well," said Pat. "Though your not remembering if you'd forgotten you'd been told about the attack is a bit worrying."

"Now I *am* confused," said Terry. "But at least I hadn't forgotten. It was the way she was phrasing it. 'Attack'. It's how I described my fading out thing to Leo when I told him about it. Now it's become his word and he's passed it on to Naomi."

They were at the kitchen table on Monday morning, a rare event as they were usually up and out to work by 7.00, breakfast gobbled on the run. Both had the morning off, no coincidence. Life needed a little slowing down occasionally, so it had become a monthly ritual to have a half-day together, stolen hours made glorious by the knowledge that their colleagues were hard at work whilst they smelt the roses.

He was telling her about Naomi's call the previous night.

"She said he'd gone after the attack. 'It finished him off,' was her actual phrase. So, I put two and two together and made nine. I thought Leo had had a heart attack and died and I'd forgotten about her ringing to tell me he wasn't well. But it was just that bloke at work. George. A verbal attack."

"Leo's mouth's always been slightly ahead of his thinking," said Pat. "What made him decide to tell this George of his feelings for him, or whatever it was?"

"It was that obsession he has with being upfront and honest about everything," said Terry. "Or, at least, when it suits him. And, I think, he also got fed up with having to go all the way round the corridors to avoid George's office. So, he told George of his attraction. George exploded and told the Dean; the Dean saw Leo and Leo resigned."

"Or didn't."

"Didn't. 'Leo's had it' turned out to mean, 'he's written a resignation letter but hasn't handed it in yet'. That's why she rang so late. He's been depressed all weekend, apparently."

"I prefer 'self-absorbed'," said Pat.

"And he put off telling Naomi for as long as he could. When he did tell her, she rang to ask me to talk him out of packing in. Which I did. It wasn't hard."

"No, I can easily believe that," said Pat. "He's a big one for the grand gesture is Leo, then he doesn't know how to get out of his unpainted corner. You gave him an easy escape route."

"Well, not that easy. I reminded him of all those times he'd talked about packing in so he could devote himself to his own creative stuff and said I admired his guts in leaving a cushy little number like that to follow his dream. That's when he started backtracking and banging on about having to get the kids through university. All that crap. He talked *himself* out of the corner."

"You're such a git," said Pat, and she laughed. "I'll tell you what I really want to know, though. How did Leo's 'fessing up to Naomi about fancying a bloke go down?"

"Good question. I must ask him. Still, it'll make a change from him banging on to her about that Dutch girlfriend he's never forgotten."

**25**

Eric Bell, the night lengthened with fitful sleep, rain hammering the roof, his thoughts a never-ending spiral, felt dazed and confused.

Ring Ernie.

Talk to Ernie.

Ernie, the only person he can talk to who he knows. All other human contact is restricted to purely functional interactions, the world a sea of passing ships.

He wonders if Ernie *has* told Camilla about him being squirrelled away in this bleak outpost. Probably. But Camilla's discreet. Trustworthy. 100% reliable. Eric would like to talk to her too but can't. His idea. He's like a deadly virus: anyone he contacts is put in danger. How did it come to this? He glances at the papers he didn't clear away. His eyes are drawn to the upwards-facing front page of the one he started to read before the wind blew out the power. A shudder goes through him.

The lights have come back on, but he didn't see it happen. He's glad he bought the blackout curtains for the bedroom window. Not that anyone is passing by. The seasonal staff are gone until March. The site owner spends his winters in Portugal.

*(Brian Yeomans was living in Portugal. Is he still? Or does he move? Or is he sparkling?)*

A security officer is supposed to drive out and patrol round the smooth tarmac roads of the park regularly, but Eric has never seen this happen in the two months he has been here.

Maybe he should have gone to Scotland after the funeral. It had been a possibility. At least there he could have walked in the street without being recognised. But then, people would inevitably start to become almost friendly. Would smile when they met him. That's why you didn't do it, he tells himself. That, and an inchoate anticipation of his current escalating, profound sense of isolation, loneliness, and despair.

He has no one here, but he does have a genetic [*genealogical?*] connection with the landscape. The big sky. All the water. The swampy wetness, green and brown and dangerous underfoot. In the fresh, salt-tinged air, the stench of his own decay is almost staunched.

Almost.

Ernie's phone is engaged. He twitches with the hyperactivity induced by his exhaustion. Ride in and see him. Get among people. He'd done that the other week and Ernie had bollocked him on the walk back down through the cemetery.

"You're out of circulation because that murdering twat expired. Now it's still your choice but if the unhinged brother sees you, it'll be permanent. Then there'll have to be a second funeral."

On the next try, five minutes later, Ernie answers straight away.

"I've been to the seaside, Ernie. I couldn't..."

"It's OK, Eric. I understand. Sit tight. I'm on my way."

# 26

Pat left for work at eleven, but Terry wasn't due in until two. He was emptying the washing-machine when the doorbell rang. It was Teresa Green. She held up a paper bag.

"Two eclairs," she said. "Put the kettle on."

He showed her where things were in the kitchen, and she made fresh coffee while he pegged the wet laundry onto the drying-rack in the bathroom.

"Good cup," he said, cramming one end of his éclair into his mouth.

"I never get why people still have instant. Beans and a grinder are a sign of evolution," she said.

"I had a friend once," said Terry through pastry. "Only twenty, both parents dead, living in a little attic room. No money but trying to move forward by getting his History degree. Every time he bought something – a book or a video or a magazine – he got rid of something else.

He was ruthless about it. He never wanted to have more things than he could carry in case he was kicked out into the street. But he always had good coffee. 'Everybody needs one luxury in their life,' he'd tell me, 'And decent coffee is mine.' It's a good philosophy."

She'd brought him a book she'd been reading, *The Suicide Machines*.

"It's about what happens when a capital city fills up and the Government doesn't know what to do with everyone, so they offer money to people to kill themselves in booths in the street."

"Sounds less far-fetched than a lot of what really goes on," said Terry.

"A friend of mine got it for me at a book-signing in town," she said. "I read it and it made me think of your pal, Eric Bell."

"Pal?" said Terry. "I never met him. How do you know his name?"

"In that book," she said, "people disappear. Eric Bell's stone is next to my husband's in the cemetery. That's near where you were lying when I found you. Pat said you'd gone to look for his grave because you thought you'd seen him in town."

"I thought I had," said Terry, "but with all these weird things happening in my head, I was probably wrong. I'm like as not going bonkers."

"You and me both then," said Teresa Green. "Because I think I've seen him as well."

## 27

As Ernie neared the coast, the storm damage was more pronounced. The road across the marsh was still flooded, the wind reluctant to let the tide back out into the firth. He diverted around crumbling B-roads that were slowly being digested by grass and weeds.

Coming around the headland, he had an oblique overview of the smashed fences, broken trees, escaping bins and the car – its owner either unaware or uncaring of the storm's power – whipped up and crookedly deposited on the vallum, never again to mow down innocent rabbits.

On the narrow access path into the caravan park, he came head-to-head with the exiting, not-after-all-mythical security van. Both drivers pulling to the left, they squeezed their vehicles by, pausing and lowering windows for the brief exchange:

"Site's shut down till the spring."

"I know but I've a nearly new 32-footer on there. Just wanted to check it."

"I've driven round. The trees kept the wind back and the drains aren't blocked up. There's no damage."

"I'll have a quick look anyway, if that's OK?"

"Please yourself."

Leaving his car in the visitor area at the main gate, Ernie laced his way on foot through the park and knocked on Eric's door. There was no reply. He knocked again and heard movement then silence. Pushing his face to the flat metal, he said,

"It's Ernie."

The door opened.

"There was a bloke here looking round. I thought you were him," said Eric.

"It was a security guard, and he was a woman and I've just passed her on the way in."

"She's coming in?"

He made to half-close the door, but Ernie put his arm out to stop him.

"*I* was coming in. *She's* gone."

Taking the view that getting Eric out of the caravan might also get some of the anxiousness out of Eric, Ernie suggested a walk round the moss at the top of the track bordering the site. And, yes, he could take the sunglasses.

They arrived at the new wooden viewing platform on the edge of the path and climbed to the top balcony. Across the flat brown expanse, shrunken by distance, were the snow-capped hills of the Northern Lakes, glistening in the newly unclouded morning sun. A flock of honking white geese arced across the landscape, disappearing behind bare trees into the bird reserve.

In the minutes it had taken to walk here from the caravan park, the wind had dropped and there was an expectant calmness in place, that false premature sense that, before too long, the days would begin to lengthen again.

Eric's words jarred with this mirage of optimism.

"I can't stand it anymore," he said, his elbows unable to gain purchase on the top of the narrow safety barrier.

He looked at Ernie in blank despair.

"You were right. I should have stayed away. Left her. Forgotten and let her forget."

Ernie placed a reassuring hand on his friend's trembling shoulder.

"We said from the start that you might not be able to see it through."

"I'm weak," said Eric.

"You're not weak. I couldn't have lasted this long without Camilla."

"You could if her safety, maybe even her life, depended on it," said Eric rubbing at his red, teary eyes.

"I've been thinking," said Ernie.

Eric turned expectantly.

"I might – *might* – have a solution."

**28**

Terry looked at the kitchen clock then at the thick envelope left by Teresa Green. He had half-an-hour before he needed to leave for work.

"You might find it interesting," she'd said without elaboration. "Let me know when you're free and we can compare conclusions."

Tempted as he was to rip open the package immediately, he washed up, packed his pannier, and went into the garage. Slipping the bag onto the bike's rear rack, he registered the slightly different feel as it clicked into place. Casting his gaze downwards, he saw the back tyre splaying out on the garage floor.

Taking the pannier off again and, with the ease of long experience, he flipped the bike upside down and set about changing the punctured inner tube. He removed the old one out and ran his thumb along the inside of the tyre, feeling the nail protruding through the rubber. By the time he'd managed to pull it out, push in the new tube, squeeze the tyre inside the wheel rim, put the wheel back between the forks, reconnect the brake and inflate the tyre, it was time to go.

He went back into the house, topped up the cat food and was just locking the back door when he heard the telephone ring in the hall. If he answered it, he'd be late. He waited and heard the answerphone click on, asking the caller to leave a message. His manager had just started to speak when Terry, Billy Whizzing across the floor, snatched the receiver from its cradle.

"Hello Sue. I was just on my way out…in. On my way in. To you."

"You need to get a mobile," said the tinny voice. "You're the only man in the whole world without one. Every other person in this building has received what is known as a text message telling them that the, and I quote, 'power outage caused by last night's storm will take time to repair and we'll be closed for the rest of the day'."

"Crikey!" said Terry. "Right."

"So don't come in," continued the voice, singing with good humour. "It's lucky I remembered and caught you just in time. Get a mobile! And keep saying,

'Crikey!' I don't want you giving up all your idiosyncrasies. Enjoy the free afternoon. See you in the morning."

He put the phone down and chuckled. Chuckling is what someone who says, 'Crikey!' does.

He looked at the envelope again. Plenty of time to examine the contents now. He picked it up, ready to open it, when low winter sunshine began streaming in through the kitchen window. Terry's spirits were always lifted by sunshine. A cloudless December sky usually presaged a frosty night, but he loved the chill of a blue afternoon. After the miserable grey weekend, it would be some kind of sin not to spend the hours till darkness riding on the cycle-path along the river.

Leaving the envelope still unopened, that's what he did.

## 29

Ernie was telling Eric about Brian Yeomans. Eric knew of him but didn't know him. Everyone in the town of a certain age knew of him, had heard the stories, the rumours, the *allegations*. He was one of Ernie's friends from the other, less visible, side of Ernie's life.

"He's been in Portugal," said Ernie. "Did I tell you that? I didn't know he was back until his grandson brought him to see me."

"You know his grandson?" said Eric.

"We connected, as they say, that day you were in the back of the shop. My bat, his fingers."

"And he brought his grandad to sort you out. That must have worried you."

"Eric, not much worries me and a lot of why I'm like that is down to Brian Yeomans. From the day I went for that job with him."

When Ernie got the interview for a job at the Grange, Brian Yeomans – the owner's only son – was in charge. This alone had been enough to make Ernie's mother tell *her* son to forget it.

"He's a dodgy bloke," she said. "The whole family's a bunch of toe-rags but Brian's the worst because he's *clever*."

She made the last word sound like an insult.

It was in catering, waiting in the restaurant. Ernie needed a job because he'd left the biscuit factory where he'd been since leaving school. There was a story.

One of the factory foremen was called Rusty Davis, a standard small man hiding behind a title. He was renowned for his systematic bullying of production liners.

Rusty's modus operandi was to point at someone then lower his finger to the floor behind him as he walked off between the belts and ovens. The unspoken expectation was that the pointee [is that a word? *The one pointed at* is a bit unwieldy] would follow the finger and, by association, Rusty to whichever area of the factory he chose. This was for no other purpose than to prove who was in charge as, on release from this magic finger, Rusty would invariably send the helpless disciples back to where'd they'd started from.

Occasionally, someone would resist the magnetic digit, resulting in a public bawling out for 'insubordination'. Further argument, it was generally accepted, would inevitably lead to instant dismissal. In those peculiar transitional days, where older workers with direct experience of a real war grafted alongside youngsters with a bourgeoning sense of liberation, a distorted discipline prevailed, and employment rights were conveniently unclear.

Ernie had avoided Rusty's psychological sadism by keeping his white-capped, hair-netted head down in Custard Creams, his machine situated in an area of the factory outside the bully's patch. It was on the second of his three days in Ginger Nuts, when Custard Creams were having their annual cleaning purge, that Ernie encountered the finger. Uncertain (but he'd heard stories) of its implications, he chose to ignore Rusty's bark and keep watching the regimented lines of biscuits as they left the oven.

The ensuing verbal tirade clarified what Ernie should do, or there'd be consequences. Ernie, manifestly unembarrassed, took the second chance kindly offered by Rusty and followed him and the pointing finger down the aisle towards Water Biscuits where, without witnesses, he knocked seven bells out of the foreman. The ambulance was just arriving as Ernie walked out of the factory gates.

He'd vaguely alluded to this 'unfortunate incident' [always good with words, Ernie, even at 18; *economical*, as with his punches] in his Grange application letter. When Brian Yeomans, unfailingly careful to interview each employee personally, asked him to elaborate, Ernie told the story straight.

"Two questions," said Brian at the conclusion. "First, do you make a habit of beating up your betters?"

"He's a bully and 'bully' trumps 'better' in my book but no, I wouldn't have touched him if he hadn't pulled out his penny-sock and swung it at me to show he was boss. There's almost always another way of sorting things out."

"Right," said Brian. "My second question. Weren't you worried he'd get the police onto you?"

"Not really," said Ernie. "Not after I mentioned that I knew where he and his wife and kids lived."

"You didn't threaten him?" said Brian.

"I never see the need. Fear's usually in people's heads," said Ernie. "You just have to make them see it."

"You got the job?" said Eric.

"I got the job," said Ernie. "Afterwards, for years, we went through a lot, me and Brian. Things that bind you together stronger than blood or money ever could. And that's why I know that, if he can, he'll help me to help you."

**30**

Terry was low on blood sugar. The ride was exhilarating but he could feel his energy levels dropping with the fading daylight. On the far side of the river, the sun was disappearing behind the Bluebell Wood. No bluebells today but they must be somewhere in the Earth, dormant, waiting. As something. A seed or bulb or other life launcher. He didn't know things that weren't there now would be there later, necessary but undesired. To desire is a human affectation in a world where life exists only to produce more life. Stop thinking. It's too cold. *Jusqu'a l'os.*

He spun into his road past walking shadows forming in the twilight.

*Moving now into the historic present* [thinking of the package].

Into the drive, into the garage, into the house. Eat a banana. Have a shower. Stroke the cat. Open the envelope. Take out the papers. They're photocopies, mainly from newspapers but some notes as well (handwritten and typed). A partial picture or two, badly reproduced. Dated [*both senses*]. Spread them all out in order on the kitchen table. Look and read.

### WOMAN DIES IN FALL FROM TRAIN

A front-page news story, a quarter of a century old. Not the original paper: nothing in the pile is original. All items were given an official police stamp, circular and indistinct, before they were copied.

The story is about a woman (unnamed) who falls to her death from a train on the coastal railway out West. Her 'boyfriend' (unnamed; pre-*partner*, this tale) tells of his grief, how the train door just came open as she leaned out for air, and somebody must pay for this avoidable tragedy. How he pulled the communication cord immediately but too late to save her. Mention is made, but not commented on, of how the fall occurred from the only high viaduct on the whole line. There were no other passengers on the train. No witnesses. Police are investigating. They will be talking to the driver (unnamed) and the train guard, **Eric Bell**.

Terry stands up and walks to the window to close the curtains. He is thinking. A woman with a small useless dog passes the house and gives a little wave. He waves back and smiles, pulls the curtains together and sits again. The next piece of paper on the pile is, it says at the top, a Witness Statement given by **Eric Bell**.

It summarises how he heard the man shouting at the woman, the smack and scream which prompted him to go to investigate what was happening, and the jerky halting of the train as the cord was pulled. It tells of how, when he reached the open door, the man wasn't showing any distress at the woman's fall. It states that, no, **Eric Bell** does not believe the woman's fall was an accident.

Burrowing through the pile, Terry discovers that the man is called **Lewis Richardson** and the dead woman **Alice Cooper**. She was young enough for her mother to have heard of the rock star but was given the name anyway. Alice had reported Richardson to police on four previous occasions for domestic violence, then dropped the charges.

Not at all sure he should be seeing any of this [official?] information, Terry reads a forensic report saying that fibres found under Richardson's fingernails correspond to those on Alice's dress. Her posthumously gathered fingerprints don't match any of the three clear sets found on the handle of the door from which she exited the train. Richardson's do.

Next in the bundle, a later newspaper giving details of Richardson's conviction and sentencing for murder, this conviction being primarily based on forensic evidence, including an expert testimony that the train door was highly unlikely to have opened on its own; and Eric Bell's witness statement, substantially repeated under oath in the trial.

The words, 'Mr Bell's evidence was possibly decisive in swaying the jury and clinching the guilty verdict' are highlighted in fluorescent pen. Richardson's 'angry vow to take revenge on Mr Bell as he was led from the court' is similarly marked.

Now, a single sheet of thin white A4 card with two news articles stapled to it: the top one tells of Lewis Richardson's successful application for parole – based on his good behaviour – whilst serving a sentence for the murder of Alice Cooper; the other, from four years ago, shorter, and smaller, the case having shrunk with time in the public imagination, reports Lewis Richardson's death at home from a suspected brain haemorrhage.

Fascinated, Terry reaches the final sheet in the pile. Another photocopied front page, from two years ago:

**MAN FEARED DROWNED IN FLOODS**

Eric Bell.

At the bottom of the copy, someone (Terry assumes it to be Teresa Green) has scribbled:

*Eric Bell disappearance. Mark Richardson connection?*

# 31

"We can go and see Brian this afternoon," said Ernie the following Thursday. "I'll come out and get you."

"I can ride in," said Eric.

"No, I'll come and get you. It'll save messing about with directions and rendezvous [*vooz* here]."

Ernie arrived at Eric's caravan just before two and they set off immediately. It was a cold afternoon, the grey sky a dustbin of snow waiting to be emptied. They didn't speak during the trip back into town because Chuck Berry was playing in the car and, as Ernie often said,

"Talking when Chuck's on is like farting in front of the Queen. Not done."

It was a view that Eric was happy to let Ernie take.

Chuck ended as they roundabouted into a 1950s housing estate with big houses and narrow roads, silent evidence of altered priorities. Ernie slowed the car and squinted as they crawled along.

"I haven't been round this place for years," said Eric. "When I was a kid, I was here all the time. We'd come up over the railway bridge across the river, a gang of us. They were still building it. It seemed exciting. One of the blokes let us have a turn driving his dumper truck. It had that weird reverse steering where you turned left and went right."

"If he did that today, he'd be arrested on at least two possible counts," said Ernie. "You can't do anything now without somebody filming it and putting it online. We're lucky we got most of our fun in before all that shite started up. It's a while since I was here as well."

Ernie slowed beside a sign and read the road name. He looked around but couldn't find a point of reference and randomly took the first left turn into a cul-de-sac. There was a paper shop at the far end. Parking outside, he disappeared into the shop. When he came out, he was carrying two ice-lollies.

"Half-price," he said. "Sales are sluggish at the moment, apparently. We must go up there."

He dropped one of the lollies into Eric's lap and the pair ate them in the time it took for the clouds to boil over and the snow to start dropping.

They pulled into Brian's drive a few minutes later, stopping alongside a small nondescript run-around and an old but well-preserved BMW. The door of the big, detached house opened, and Brian Yeomans appeared, waving them in before disappearing back inside. The two men got out and followed him into a spacious, immaculate hallway.

"Brian," said Ernie. "You know Eric."

Brian didn't really but covered his unfamiliarity smoothly.

"Eric," he said, shaking his hand. "It's been a long time. Let's go into the lounge."

They divided between the two armchairs and the small sofa arranged in a triangle and sat down. Brian eased back and looked at Ernie, a signal for him to start speaking.

"Lewis Richardson," said Ernie and Eric saw Brian Yeomans's eyes spark into life.

"Ah. Eric," he said. "That Eric. The man who put Lewis away for doing Alice Cooper. I knew her mother, God rest her. Got it."

"He was let out," said Ernie. "Seven years ago."

"He hasn't waited this long to get his own back?" said Brian. "He hasn't got the patience. Neither's his psycho brother."

"Lewis is dead," said Ernie. "Brain haemorrhage."

"No loss there," said Brian.

Ernie motioned to Eric.

"Tell Brian the rest."

Eric tensed then launched into his story.

"When Lewis was taken down, he swore he'd get me for giving evidence against him. Even though it was the forensics that showed he'd killed her. The police told me to forget it because he'd forget it. They said if he came after me when he got out or anything happened to me while he was still in, they'd push for his parole to be revoked. They said he had a long history of making empty threats."

"But not empty in your case?" said Brian.

"Thirteen years ago, my solicitor told me he was pushing for early release and, because he'd behaved himself, was likely to get it."

"How did you feel about that?" said Brian.

"If it had just been me, I'd have taken my chances, but I had a wife and two teenagers. So, I applied for a transfer from my job down to Lancashire. Told Carol I fancied a change, a new challenge, and she was happy enough to go along. Didn't tell her the real reason. Anyway, I got it and off we went. Didn't need to tell anybody where we were going except for the family and Ernie here. Ernie was the only one knew I was worried and, well you know him, he didn't feed me any of that, *'it'll be alright,'* bullshit. Said I was doing the right thing in the circumstances."

Eric looked at Ernie who was gently nodding his head.

"You knew Lewis, Brian," said Ernie. "Complete nut-job."

"Mmm," said Brian. "Go on."

"We moved away, got the kids through school and off to other parts as soon as they were old enough. They've both got families now. When I knew they were alright, I thought about moving back up here with Carol. Home.

Richardson got out the year after we went South but had gone to live near Stirling. I reckoned we were OK so talked Carol round. I was ready to pack in the railway anyway. We sold up for a good price down there and bought in the middle of that big estate past the cemetery. Where nobody would find us, I thought…"

Eric stopped talking and started running his hand through his hair, the stress signifier that Ernie knew so well. His eyes seemed to have lost focus, were beginning to water. His breathing was accelerating. Ernie moved across to him.

"Steady, Eric. You're nearly done. Nearly done. Finish telling your story to Brian, and we can see if he's got any ideas."

<h1 style="text-align:center">32</h1>

Terry was hoping to see Teresa Green the day after she left him the envelope but needed to make up the time lost at work due to the power cut. He had to wait until Thursday evening, the same day Eric went to see Brian.

Pat invited her for tea.

"She lives on her own. It'll be nice for her to have a meal cooked for a change. You can do her one of your curry things."

On his way home on Wednesday, he stopped off at Lidl for shopping. He was looking at the newly arrived Christmas goodies when he felt a tap on his shoulder.

"I'd like you to accompany me to the manager's office please, sir."

"Hello Dennis," Terry said, turning and smiling. "I didn't think you were allowed out on your own. Which marzipan is better: original or Rum and Raisin?"

"Pineapple," said Dennis, snatching one up from the shelf and sniffing at it. "I'm glad I've run into you, Terry. I need to come and see you and Pat about the garage conversion. I can probably start on it early January."

As they ran through some possible dates, a man and woman came up and stood beside them.

"This is Jim and his partner Fiona," said Dennis.

"I'm Dennis's oldest friend," said Jim, shaking Terry's hand. "We were at school together."

"Pleased to meet you," said Terry, hiding his surprise. "I'm Terry, as Dennis didn't say. He's not my friend but we're sort of mutually dependent. Hello Fiona."

Terry's surprise was at the thought of Dennis and Jim being the same age. Whilst Dennis oozed strength and vigour, Jim was one of those men who appears old at first sight then, when you look closer, isn't but has been worn down by life. His hair was prematurely grey, and he was thin, but his thinness was punctuated by a little beer belly ballooning over his waistband. His hand was soft, and his handshake lacked any energy. Terry thought it unlikely he was a manual worker.

Fiona looked as old as Dennis but was probably just as young. She was slim (no beer belly), of medium height and had light brown hair that may or may not have been natural. She shared Dennis's weary demeanour, but it was augmented by a look Terry couldn't put his finger on. *Haunted*, perhaps.

As was often the case when someone was introduced as a 'partner', Terry couldn't stop himself from speculating on what the back story was. You knew where you were when people were married (even unhappily) but, in people past a certain age, 'partner', in Terry's view, was a word that indicated a degree of ambivalence. Intrigue, even.

"Jim and Fiona live just outside Manchester," said Dennis, "but they're staying with us for a couple of days, so I've brought them to see the bright lights of Lidl."

"Hasn't Lidl reached the wilds of Manchester yet then?" said Terry.

(Pat often told him to be careful with his irony, especially with people he'd just met who didn't *know his sense of humour*. "And don't let it spill over into sarcasm.")

"Oh yes, but I've never been in one," said Fiona *without irony*. "We prefer Sainsbury's, don't we Jim?"

Jim made a non-committal noise, which Terry madly interpreted as shorthand for, '*I don't give a shit where we shop, and it makes me look like a knob to be the other bit of the 'We' in 'We prefer…' but anything for a quiet life.*'

"I don't expect they have soya milk in here," Fiona again, "but we're lactose-intolerant."

"They do actually," said Dennis who, knowing Terry well, had figured out what he was probably thinking about Fiona. "It's over there. Hang on here with Terry a minute, Jim."

Jim watched them go in silence, a quiet intensity enveloping him, as if his thoughts were suddenly somewhere else completely. After a moment, Terry pointed at the marzipan and said,

"Original or Rum and Raisin? Or pineapple?"

But Jim was still bewitched and didn't reply. '*Maybe he thinks Fiona and Dennis are having a fling,*' thought Terry but only because his mind had to fill the void with something. In any case, Dennis completely adored *his* wife, so the thought was completely stupid.

"Have you known Fiona long?" said Terry, trying again.

"For years at work," said Jim, but much more to himself than to Terry. "God, I hope this Christmas will be OK for her.

[*Pause*]

She hates Christmas because it always reminds her.

[*Pause. A longer one.*]

It was Christmas Eve four years ago when her husband shot himself."

'*There's really no answer to that*,' thought Terry, relieved at the sight of Dennis and Fiona returning triumphantly, soya milk in hand.

# 33

Back to the day after, and Eric's sweating palm is leaving fading dark streaks across one arm of Brian Yeomans's burgundy leather sofa. Ernie is saying,

"Steady, Eric. You're nearly done. Nearly done. Finish telling your story to Brian, and we can see if he's got any ideas."

Eric rubbed his hands down his trousers and continued.

"I packed in the job down there and we moved back up into the new house. Carol had been working at a hairdresser's. She's a good cutter so got plenty of work here, filling in at a place in town when the proper chairs took their days off. A unisex place. Well, they all have the same cuts nowadays, with all that gender fluidity stuff…"

"I blame The Rolling Stones," said Ernie, rolling his eyes.

"Anyhow," said Eric, momentarily annoyed, "I went to the shop one night to pick her up after work and she's the last cutter in there, finishing off this bloke who's maybe 40 and having one of those rockabilly sides short, top quiff cuts. I sit down to wait for her, reading a magazine. The bloke goes, Carol sweeps up, locks the shop and we go for the bus. We get off and, as the bus pulls away, something makes me look at it. In the back seat is Rockabilly and our eyes lock, just for a split-second then he's gone. I don't recognise him but what I saw in that brief look was pure hatred. The next morning…"

After Carol went to work the next morning, Eric decided to cut the grass. It was a promising summer's day, the little cloud there was chased off by a warming breeze, and Eric was ready for some physical exertion.

He unlocked the shed in the back garden and pulled out the ancient push-mower. Giving the rusty blade an optimistic squirt of lubricant, he guided it up the gravel path along the side of the house and positioned it on the front lawn. He nodded at a passer-by walking a tall spindly dog then went back down to the shed for the metal collection box that clipped onto the mower.

It wasn't hanging on its usual hook, and this puzzled him because he could have sworn it had been there a couple of minutes earlier. He looked around the small shed, but the box had definitely gone. A wave of disappointment ran through him at the thought that there was someone in this pleasant, welcoming neighbourhood who was stealing. The second unstoppable wave reminded him that he was in no position to be a hypocrite but, then again, appropriating the odd thing (*watches!*) from a huge warehouse wasn't the same. Wasn't *personal*.

As he turned and stepped out of the shed back into the garden, it hit him. Literally. Not figuratively.

The box came at him from nowhere and glanced off his right temple. Eric slithered down onto the grass like a board-game snake, green flakes of metal paint swirling around and onto him as he fell. Though stunned, he retained enough awareness to feel the cut above his eye made by a jagged shard of steel on the lip of the box as it rebounded off his head.

He lay on the grass on his back and carefully touched the cut. Trying to focus on his bloody finger, he felt the sun go out and looked up to the sky. A dark outline, the cause of the eclipse, loomed above him.

"Hello Eric," it said. "It is you, isn't it?"

Eric was trying to think fast but the world around him was moving too slowly.

"No..." he began.

"Oh, it wasn't a proper question, Eric. It's what's called a *rhetorical* enquiry. To create a dramatic effect rather than to get an answer. I already know it's you. And you know me, don't you?"

"I... I can't think. Hurts. Why you hit me?"

In response, the shadow of the mower box came down, down, down, down again, flattening the grass around Eric's head, then stopping.

Eric, half-unconscious with the combination of blows and fright, tried to get up. He rolled himself onto his front, splayed his hands out on the ground and pushed. His large frame barely moved until the freezing water hit him. He jerked up and rolled over again, eyes heavy, his heart thumping, the cut feeling like it was boring into the centre of his brain. The nozzle of the hosepipe entered his mouth, its tight jet filling his throat. He couldn't cough and knew he would drown. Then the water stopped, and he felt the nozzle withdraw.

He became aware that the weight on each shoulder was caused by the knees of the man straddling him. Rockabilly from the bus.

"You know me," said Rockabilly.

"Don't," said Eric, his tongue running around a newly loose tooth.

"Guess."

There was only one real possibility: Lewis Richardson. But if it was, he'd changed his appearance.

"Guess," said Rockabilly. "Or we'll give you another little drink."

"Lewis. You're Lewis Richardson," said Eric.

"WRONG!" said Rockabilly seizing Eric's hair and forcing his head up. "One more try."

Eric was puzzled. Who else could it be?

"His brother?" he said, in the absence of any other inspiration.

"Brilliant," said Rockabilly. "My name is Mark. Remember it. My brother is dead, and you helped kill him. Prison did for Lewis, I know it, and he was there because of you. So, it'll be your turn soon. But not till you've suffered a bit. You and your lovely wife."

"Mark Richardson," said Brian Yeomans. "The best advert for reviving the Massacre of the Innocents I can think of. Oh dear."

<h1 style="text-align:center">34</h1>

She put down her fork after one mouthful.

"Delicious, but I can't eat it."

"Why not?" said Terry.

"Don't ask rude questions," said Pat.

"I don't mind," said Teresa Green. "It's got nuts in it and I'm allergic to them. Sorry. I didn't think to say. But you eat yours."

"Are you OK with cheese salad?" said Pat.

She nodded and tried but failed to stop Pat going out into the kitchen. Terry looked across at her.

"Well," she said. "What do you think?"

"That Eric Bell used the floods to fake his own death."

"Why?"

"Because he thought Lewis Richardson was dead and it was safe to move back up here but Lewis found him and threatened him and likely his wife. It would be the wife he was most worried about."

"Lewis *is* dead," said Teresa Green. "Did you not see the article I put in the pile?"

"Yes, but I thought…"

"You think everybody's faking their own deaths?"

"Then if not Lewis, who?"

"His brother, Mark. I made a note. He took on the role of avenging angel after Lewis died."

"But it was the forensic stuff that put Lewis in jail. Eric's evidence was a small nail in an already sealed coffin."

"You can't take revenge on lab tests," said Teresa Green. "But you can on a man."

"So, what do we do with our conclusions?" said Terry.

"There's nothing to do," said Teresa Green. "The only one who can make anything happen is Eric Bell himself."

Later, when Pat was taking Teresa home, Terry thought about the story so far. It was interesting and engrossing but ultimately impermanent. He might see Eric Bell again, but Teresa was right: people have to sort out their own lives.

The part of tonight's discussion which had made the biggest impression on him, he realised, was Lewis Richardson's death. The manner of it. A brain haemorrhage. Or an aneurysm. Terry had seen Eric Bell but now – and he knew it was a crazy notion – he really wanted to see the late Lewis Richardson. To ask him if he'd had any *mental episodes* which in any way resembled his own.

He was sitting reading as Pat returned.

"What's the book?"

"*Biggles Flies East*."

"Pretty heavy for a lecturer in English Literature."

"Which I'm not," he said, just before a dark monster swallowed him.

<h1 style="text-align:center">35</h1>

Eric Bell stared at Ernie Fox and Brian Yeomans.

"You'd have to give the life insurance back," said Ernie.

"Carol got it. She might have bought that house she's living in with it. But the old house could sell if it gets another push after Christmas and that would cover it."

"Have a think about the Mark Richardson problem and let me know if you want it dealt with," said Brian Yeomans.

"Thanks Brian," said Ernie. "We'll be in touch."

After the unenthusiastic snowfall earlier, the roads were wet and dirty but at least all the ice had disappeared. Ernie and Eric drove back out to the coast, this time without music.

"What would he do? If I said yes, I mean?"

"Whatever it takes to sort out your problem. Brian has what might be called 'reach'. He knows everybody and a lot of people owe him favours. His big strength though, which I only have in a limited way, is that he doesn't care."

"Evil then," said Eric.

"No. He's neither good nor bad. He just does what must be done without worrying about consequences. First time I saw that was just after I started that job at the Grange."

"'Fear's usually in people's heads. You just have to make them see it.' Great answer."

It was what clinched the job for Ernie, impressed Brian Yeomans, made Brian think even then that Ernie had the right stuff.

The job, at the start, was as advertised. Basically, a waiter, though Ernie was always willing to help out in the kitchen or behind the bar if required. Most people weren't. Or couldn't. Inflexible. To Brian Yeomans, this meant they *didn't* have the right stuff. But that was OK, so long as they got on with whatever limited work they were capable of. From the start, though, Ernie demonstrated flexibility.

The Grange itself was a former stately home situated in a couple of acres of land five miles to the East of the town. Its rural setting coupled with its accessibility made it a popular choice for wedding receptions, particularly among those who Brian summarily referred to as having 'wallets even thicker than their ugly heads'.

Brian's dad, so the stories went, had acquired it at a knockdown price from the previous owner through his possession of photographs of the man pleasuring himself with large farm animals.

As well as the ballroom where the weddings were held, there were 22 bedrooms, a bar and a swimming-pool with a small gym attached. The restaurant, where Ernie was based, also functioned as a weekend disco for the area's car-mobile youths; a cabaret club for occasional visits from former big names on the fade; and, from time to time, a casino. Again, given how notoriously frugal the local council was with its granting of gaming licences, rumours circulated as to what kinds of information Yeomans Senior held on decision makers at the Town Hall, but nothing of this was ever made public.

Brian had taken over the Grange when the inherited manager left for the Costa with a safeful's worth of takings. Brian's father sent his son out to Spain to retrieve the man and the money, partly to see if the chip was as ruthless and efficient as the old block. It was, Brian returning with a suitcase of English banknotes and a wheelchair carrying what was left of the absconder. Brian passed the test and got to keep the cash, the amount involved providing sufficient evidence of the long-term potential gains to be had from running the place.

Ernie's initial observations were that Brian's approach to management duties was distinctly hands-off, most of the practicalities of running a hotel being delegated to Cheryl, his assistant manager and also, allegedly, his part-time bed warmer.

Where he really came into his own, however, was when higher-order people skills were required. He could usually schmooze his (and his staff's) way out of any problems that arose with the wide range of clients who patronised the Grange. However, if his considerable charm did fail to win them round, he would introduce subtly menacing hints as to what might befall anyone who persisted in behaving unreasonably.

About three weeks after Ernie started working there, the incident that would forever change his relationship with his boss took place.

Brian, who relished his life at the Grange, had taken a rare night off to accompany his father to what wasn't then called a networking event with the local greats and goods. He left Cheryl in charge and an emergency phone number where he could be reached. Ernie, meanwhile, was on his own in the restaurant, setting up for a gambling extravaganza of roulette, blackjack, and various types of poker when he spotted a large black car prowling up the drive towards the main building.

It was an early summer's evening, the light just starting to fade, but Ernie could see what was happening. The car stopped and two men got out of the front seats. They opened the back doors on either side and two more men, in hats and unseasonal but obviously expensive overcoats, also got out. When this pair produced cigarettes, the others began scrabbling to light them, which showed Ernie how the power was dispersed within the group.

As the four stood on the gravel looking around, a member of the hotel's gardening staff went by, pushing a wheelbarrow filled with soil. For no obvious reason, one of the non-smoking pair took off his hat, placed it on the car roof then ran at the wheelbarrow, kicking it over. The gardener, clearly shocked, righted it then began to throw the sods back in as the four men looked on, laughing. When he finished, the same man kicked it over again.

Ernie could see the gardener start to remonstrate with the man, who put his hand inside his overcoat and pulled something part of the way out. At this, the gardener abandoned barrow and soil and took off. Ernie couldn't see what the man had in his hand, but he had a fair idea.

The scene ended and Ernie realised that Cheryl had come into the restaurant at some point and was also watching.

"What the fuck was that about?" she said. "I'm going to sort that twat out."

She made to move but Ernie put a restraining hand on her shoulder.

"I think that was a gun he had. Do you know where to contact Mr Yeomans?"

When Brian Yeomans arrived, it was just after eight and now completely dark. He clocked the visitors making themselves loudly comfortable in the lounge bar (which was emptying fast) before going to find Cheryl in the restaurant. She repeated what she'd told him on the phone, including Ernie's gun theory.

"Ernie," said Brian. "Can you come here?"

Ernie, who had been trying to be discreet, put down the tablecloth and walked over.

"Yes, Mr Yeomans?"

"How would you feel about asking our guests how you might be of assistance to them? You can tell them I sent you to ask."

"OK," said Ernie without hesitation.

"What about the gun?" said Brian.

"We'll see," said Ernie, grinning.

"I'll follow at a distance. They don't know who I am, but I recognise the two in charge. Any trouble, you just walk away."

"Who are they?" said Cheryl.

"The Lewthwaites. Robbie and Ricky."

"The gangsters?" said Cheryl. "From London? Can't be. What would they be doing up here?"

"We might find out in a minute. Can you go and get Billy and Harry from estates, just in case? Ready, Ernie?"

He nodded and the pair walked across the gravel to the lounge, Brian pausing at the door to let Ernie enter alone. He went up to the four and did what Brian had asked.

"How can you be of assistance?" said one of the pair who'd been in the back of the car. Either Robbie or Ricky. "What do you think, boys? What can this fine young lad do to help us?"

"He could suck on this," said the barrow-kicker, his hand going to his trouser zip as he stood up.

"Nah. This is better," said the other lackey who, as he also got up, pulled out a gleaming black handgun and pushed it at Ernie's mouth.

Without missing a beat, Ernie swatted the gun away with his left hand and hit the man in the stomach with his right. As he went over, the barrow-kicker also brought out a gun and pointed it at Ernie, who sidestepped and headbutted him before stamping on his recovering colleague's hand.

The two Lewthwaites were just starting to understand what was happening when Billy and Harry ran in and wrestled them to the ground. Brian Yeomans, meanwhile, wandered over and casually kicked the two guns away.

"Pond," he said, ignoring the profanity-loaded threats now issuing loudly from the four.

An hour later, soaked and smelling of dank water, the visitors were deposited onto the concourse at the railway station, all traces of threat and bravado knocked out of them.

"The last train to London goes in 25 minutes. You'd better buy tickets," said Brian Yeomans, only the second time he'd spoken to them.

"The car," said a Lewthwaite.

"Yes, thanks for that. It'll cover the cost of the drinks you didn't pay for," said Brian.

"You…," started one of the lackeys.

Brian put a finger to his lips before pointing to the platform where the 25 to 30 men he'd summoned had gathered to guarantee the four got on the train.

"The Lewthwaites?" said Eric Bell. "Up here? You expect me to believe that?"

"It's that Whatsisname the film star thing," said Ernie. "When people recognised him and asked, 'What are you doing here?' he'd always reply, 'I've gotta be somewhere.'"

"And what *were* they doing up here?"

"Brian reckoned they were on their way back from doing business in Glasgow and stopped off for a bit of fun. Or to try and squeeze a bit of money. Both probably. We never found out."

"Didn't they come back?"

"For what?"

"The car, if nothing else."

"They wouldn't have got it, then that would have been twice they'd been shown up by hicks from the sticks."

"But…the Lewthwaites."

"Just a name," said Ernie. "Only be scared when you've got something *real* to be scared about. Something close to home. Like Mark Richardson."

<h1 align="center">36</h1>

Terry could see the top of the jockey's cap, where the red and white sections met beneath a little white button. He was wearing a similarly coloured gilet and black trousers or leggings, or whatever it is that jockeys wear. The horse's colour was hard to work out as most of its body was lost beneath the swirling grey fog. Maybe piebald, or was that just a guess?

The pair seemed to be moving fast but it was hard to tell because there were no other riders to compare progress with. *Should they even be running a race in these conditions?* Terry wondered. Where was the finish line? *Helsinki?*

*There's ink in Hell? no wonder it's dark but it isn't, it's yellow and hot like a jaundiced model...* One final look back and ᵁᴾ at Terry and the fog took over and all he could do was focus on the afterimage, what had been there, was still there [*was it?*] but lost from view.

The jockey's face was his face. Terry's face. The face of Terry. Terry watching Terry riding a horse that was his own body. No, not body, *brain*. Riding the brain so that the brain could then guide the body. Like a big Numskull. The brain going into the fog, taking the body into the fog, letting it stumble and fall and disappear.

*I'm gone*, thought Terry.

But he wasn't.

He woke up in a hospital room that was very like the previous hospital room except this one had four other beds in it, all showing signs of occupancy but all currently empty. He saw machinery and tubes around him and tried to push his head further up the pillow to see what they were connected to, but he couldn't.

There was something in his right hand, he could feel that, could his middle finger trace its outline? work out what it was? very hard to make the finger wake, wake finger, move, no fine motor skills, only. Gross. Stabbing, jabbing down onto a metal disc in his palm. The pain in his head. That's not nice. That's burning my brain. That wasn't fog I saw; it was smoke from the fire *burning my brain.*

He felt the metal disc move infinitesimally, thought he heard a far-off ship's siren, closed his eyes. Next thing you know, there's *somebody touching my shoulder and I've to go to the trouble of raising my eyelids again, worra pain. In my head.*

"Terry? Terry? Did you press your alarm?"

He managed the eyelid reopening and there was a face floating between a white cap and a blue uniform, the three parts eventually coalescing, *that's a nurse, what's my prize for spotting that?*

The nurse called the doctor, who arrived as the sedative began to take effect and Terry's body stopped convulsing.

"Terry? Can you hear me?"

"No," said Terry, his voice a slur.

"He's making jokes. That's a good sign. When did he wake up?"

"About an hour ago now. I buzzed you right away."

"Terry? Can you see the light of the torch? Follow the light with your eyes. Good. Very good."

"He's falling asleep. The sedative's kicking in properly."


*Voices are disappearing down a well. A silo. A metal silo. 'Heartbreak Hotel' was recorded inside a metal silo. That's why it's got such a great echo… echo… echo… echo… echo…*

## 37

Eric Bell couldn't decide what to do. He knew he wasn't a brave man though he'd done brave things. If 'brave' was the word to describe his petty fencing of the watches.

The watches.

They'd been in the lock-up for months and Walter wasn't coming back for them, not after the stroke. He'd told Eric that himself, sluggishly and not always clearly, with that changed voice, the slowed-down tape-recorder voice, the heavy finger on the spinning vinyl voice, the stretched cassette tape voice, the any-old-technology-not-working-properly voice. A broken analogue voice that couldn't be repaired because no one made the spare parts anymore.

"I got 20 boxes," he told Eric when Eric went to visit him in the home.

"One every week just about for the six months I was on the Edinburgh run. Twenty-four watches in each box. Good uns. They piled them in the guard's van at the Birmingham end and they were collected at the other. At least a hundred boxes in every shipment. They weren't going to miss the odd one. Sell them. It'll pay for treats for the family."

He gave Eric the key and the address and Eric had some notion of gathering the proceeds and giving them to Walter's wife, but she couldn't manage without a strong, fit Walter who'd always done everything for her. She died six months after his left side stopped functioning properly and he followed before the year was out.

Eric, with his nearly 500 watches. Good uns. Ten at a time pinned inside his works jacket. Or in the red plastic box he took down the club on a Friday. He'd played it slowly, never tried to force them onto anybody.

"Don't be pushy and don't be greedy," Walter had said.

Good advice.

They had bought six or seven months' worth of little treats: cinema trips; summer ice creams; occasional meals out; that big television. And given Eric Bell perhaps the only spell of good luck he'd ever had as, when the watches stopped working – as they quickly did – almost no one asked for their money back. They understood that they were complicit.

Had he been brave? Approaching people, some complete strangers, to see if they wanted to buy knock-off watches that had turned out not to be *good* but *shoddy crap*?

He'd gone to help the girl, Alice Cooper. He'd only listened to that psycho Richardson shouting at her for 10 minutes before he got up off his fat arse in his nice warm guard's office [hideout!] with the intention of… doing what? When the train braked and he'd fallen over *he knew* he hadn't really intended to go all the way up to the errant lovers, *knew* he'd have stopped halfway and considered his own safety and gone back to his *hideout*.

His self-disgust at not saving her found some atonement in his statement to the police. It was his lurch at redemption, doing it for Alice, doing it for his self-respect. Not deviating from his story that he believed Lewis Richardson had helped the girl out of the train. Very brave and look where it had taken him. And Carol.

Now he, Eric Bell, had another chance. Lewis had gone but he could, if he chose, have Brian Yeomans expunge Nutty Boy Mark Richardson from this world. He could have Carol back and they could take up from where they'd left off, though probably without the house they'd have to sell to pay back the life policy. Unless he was done for wasting police time or defrauding an insurance company or pretending to be dead when he wasn't. [Is that a crime?].

If he went to prison, he and Carol still wouldn't be together. He'd no longer be in hiding, of course, but even his present existence, creeping around the edges of others' normal lives, was preferable to being confined. And what if he ended up in a place filled with the Richardsons' cronies [if they had any, but they must, that kind sticks together] and one of them decided to take revenge on behalf of the poor misunderstood brothers who never had a proper chance in life?

The more he thought about it, the less able he was to focus. He also knew that he was avoiding the big elephant in the room that was his head: what if Carol didn't want him back?

"I'll give it till Saturday and decide then," he told Ernie on the phone. "Don't let me put it off any longer than that."

## 38

The consultant neurologist would see Terry on her Friday morning ward round. He'd been in hospital for a little over thirteen hours. She'd read the duty doctor's report from the night before as well as details of his previous incident. She'd looked at the MRI scan results. She was at something of a loss.

"Can we get a test done asap?" she said to her colleague in clinical psychology. "If you take a look first, I'll move him to last on my list. See if we can come up with anything between us."

Terry was awake and alert when the psychologist arrived at 8.50. The pain in his head had gone and he'd eaten a healthy [as in *big* not *balanced*] breakfast. He'd rung Pat and told her he felt fine [*again, like the last time then look what happened, stay there until they find something this time otherwise the next one might kill you or paralyse you, I don't want to put ideas in your head, but I'm worried about you, I love you…*].

"Terry? My name is Jane Shepherd. I'm a psychologist based here in the hospital. I'd just like to ask you a few questions. Is that OK?"

He nodded and switched off the television above his bed. You paid to watch television in hospital except between 7.30 a.m. and noon when you had free, unlimited access to the five main terrestrial channels. Not much of a viewer at any time, Terry had been flicking between programmes with a growing sense of fascination as repeats of old US sitcoms vied with dumbed-down news programmes and vicious laugh-at-a-cretin shows for audience share. It wasn't for him, but he supposed it served some sort of purpose.

Each to their own.

The first few questions were perfunctory identity-checkers. He watched himself smiling at Jane Shepherd smiling at him, ashamed because he suspected her friendly demeanour masked an underlying insincerity. She moved on to mental arithmetic.

"Apples are 70p a bag. You have a £2 coin. How many bags can you buy?"

"Two."

"And how much change do you need?"

"60p."

"I make it 40p."

"Then it's a good job you're a doctor and not a shopkeeper. I'm not confused or forgetful or impaired. I feel completely normal."

When the neurologist appeared just before lunchtime, Terry was reading a copy of *1984* he'd taken from the trolley of the weekly book exchange volunteer. A story about a future that was itself now in the past, it brought on a familiar mental trope of Terry's of Time not being linear; of events as a series of floating spheres that randomly came into view, collided, and floated off again but never disappeared. Of *randomness* and *linear* being words conjured up to try and explain the ineffable. Beyond the capability of human understanding.

[The finite mind cannot comprehend infinity *and we're all in a little submarine*.]

"How are you feeling?" she said.

[Shall I tell her I can't stop thinking, can't slow my brain, it's looping, not in order; you think The Incredible Shrinking Man will disappear, but he just goes sub-atomic; religious faith is inconsistent with Fallibilism; Karl Popper just popped out…?]

"I feel good," said Terry, immediately regretting the *good*, it being antithetical to his nature. "OK, anyway. Like after the first attack, I feel rested."

She was looking at him curiously, the notes from the end of his bed in her hand, the top sheet (of paper, not bed linen) half-turned.

"We can't find anything wrong," she said. "Scans are clear, there's no sign of physical or psychological impairment and sensory responses are normal."

"Do you ever wonder what 'normal' is?" said Terry before he could stop himself.

"Do you?" she said, her brow furrowing slightly.

He held up the novel.

"Depends on where you live. And when. When you smile, when you smile at me…"

He shut up and shrugged his shoulders.

"Can I go home? Don't want to be a bed-blocker."

She had a cautious expression on her face, as if trying to fathom something half-forgotten.

"There's something not right here Terry," she said. "We both know it, but we don't know what it is. I get the feeling you're…what's the word? Drifting. Inside your head. Thinking too much. Does that make sense to you?"

It did and he nodded, his eyes moving down to the blue tiled floor, tears welling up.

"Have you someone you can call to take you home?"

He nodded again, feeling blank and utterly forlorn. She stood up and put her hand on his shoulder.

"I'm going to help you," she said.

They could hear his anguished wailing down in the atrium below.

# 39

It was two years since the latest floods and some people still weren't back in their homes. The devastation was particularly shocking because similar storms a decade earlier were seen as exceptional, a 'once in every 200 years' occurrence.

This time, the bad weather began on the middle Friday of December as an unpredicted change of wind direction over the Atlantic drove cold air and torrential rain up against the West coast.

When it started, Eric Bell was at his wits' end. For seven months, true to his word, Mark Richardson had been conducting a misguided revenge against him for sealing his brother's murder conviction. Mark was convinced that Lewis's demise in a public car-park – the expiry time on the ticket he'd just bought proving to be later than his own – was a direct consequence of the stress he experienced in prison.

A broad overview of the myriad factors that contributed to Lewis's sentencing would have shown that Eric Bell's evidence formed a small part of the prosecution's case, but this didn't interest Mark. He *knew* that Eric had killed Lewis as surely as if he'd plunged a sharp knitting needle into his ear.

Mark's image.

After the initial vicious assault in the garden, nothing happened for weeks. Eric blamed the damage to his head and face on an unfortunate stumble over an uneven flagstone. Carol had bought the story, at least at first, but Ernie wasn't fooled for a second.

"Lewis Richardson's brother? Mad Mark? He's trouble. He's unhinged. I'll help you sort him if anything else happens but the family's big, vanya everybody on the estate."

The follow-up incidents, when they came, were small but disturbing: scratches along the side of the car; a brick through the back kitchen window; dog shit smeared over the outside door handles. It was when the garden shed burnt down that Eric started to really worry. Carol wanted to report it to the police, but Eric put it down to the dodgy electrical supply.

His concerns began to ramp up just after Halloween when Carol arrived home early from work one afternoon. Eric was upstairs, putting washing away, when he heard the front door burst open and her scream his name. Rushing downstairs, she'd collapsed into his arms.

"Oh Eric, you're here. This bloke came in the shop looking for me. He told me you'd had an accident and the police, and an ambulance were here. You'd fallen off the roof. I ran all the way…"

The 'he' wasn't Mark Richardson as Eric assumed. That was cleared up the next morning when Rockabilly Mark himself appeared at the front door.

"Did my mate get your wife into a sweat yesterday, Eric? Did she think you were injured? Well, this is to tell you that that was the practice run. The real thing'll be along soon. What I can't decide is whether to do something to her first. Not that I've anything personal against her. She does a lovely cut and is a very nice lady but, unfortunately for her, she's your big weak spot. I'd make sure you saw it happen."

He turned to walk away.

"What can I do?" said Eric. "To make you lay off."

"You can't do anything, Eric, short of dying yourself. And you can't go to the police because if you do, I'll have someone onto her straight away. I'll be in touch again very soon."

After a week of thinking about it, Eric went to see Ernie.

"So, I've no option. I'm gonna have to disappear. For Carol's sake."

"I'll sort him out," said Ernie.

"No," said Eric. "All that'll achieve is getting the whole Richardson family after both of us. And Carol and Camilla."

"There was a time when I could have taken them all on," said Ernie.

Eric squeezed Ernie's arm.

"You're a wise man, Ernie," said Eric, "and a wise man knows his limitations."

"When and how will you vanish?" said Ernie.

"Soon," said Eric. "I'll make it look good. Keep an eye out for Carol. I'll lie low for a bit then get in touch but don't tell anybody. Not even Camilla."

Ernie instantly dismissed this last sentence but said,

"Let me help you, Eric. When you're ready."

Eric Bell spent early November looking for a place where he could hide after he made his move. It had to be outside the town, quiet and somewhere he wouldn't be known. He considered relocating further away but it held no appeal. This was his part of the world and he suspected he'd need an emotional attachment to something when he quit his normal life.

A conversation with a neighbour complaining of having to vacate his holiday caravan for three months every winter gave him the idea.

Eric visited several sites before he happened on the one out on the firth. Making enquiries, he found that its main customers came from the North-East rather than being local. It added another layer of potential concealment.

He put down a deposit on a decent second-hand 32-footer, promised to abide by the 'no winter residency' requirement, then set up a manageable monthly payment from an account in the name of George Stephenson. The account contained £25,000 he'd won on the Premium Bonds. He'd told no one about it, intending to use the money to take Carol on a surprise dream holiday. Now that wouldn't happen and, moreover, the money was forever tainted by association with his imminent disappearance.

Every step of this secret planning process caused him agony. He hated himself, his deceptiveness, his lying to Carol about the great Christmas they'd have… Dodgy watches and the Premium Bonds win aside, lying wasn't in his nature but it was the only way out he could see.

When he had the second, brief doorstep visit from Mark Richardson – "Don't bother ordering a turkey this year," being his only words – he knew it was time to make his move.

On the Saturday morning, two days after the December storms started, Carol was at work. Eric, worn down by yet another sleepless night, left her a note saying he was going to look at the swollen waterfall beside the cycle-path. Forcing himself to walk out of the house for the last time, he set off on his clanky bike down to the Holmes as the storm continued to build.

By the time he reached the riverbank, the wind was at its height. Eric could see only one other person braving the elements and they were in the far distance, L-bent and heading away from him.

Furtively, he placed the bike in the surging water, jammed it strategically between the roots of an old fallen tree where it was sure to be noticed, then set off up through the trees to the bridleway at the top of Jollyboys Hill.

As arranged, Ernie was waiting for him in his mud-splattered old car. Eric slid into the passenger seat and the two headed for the coast, the car rocking against the now-driving rain. Buffeted by the gale, the falling branches and swirling debris on the road seemed to echo Eric's inner turmoil.

# 40

Meanwhile, Terry, unable to cycle against the same Saturday afternoon winds, walked into town with Pat. When she peeled off to meet her friend, he carried on down towards the castle. Curving over the hill leading to the sports centre, he saw the 'Closed' signs blocking off the big roundabout that was the hub for major transport routes in every direction. As muddy brown water lapped around the tops of the traffic lights leading onto it, council workers in orange jackets and police in fluorescent green puzzled over how to manage the devastation.

He walked past the local BBC radio station.

"Every cloud," he said to himself as he watched the illuminated red sign above the entrance swinging erratically.

Local radio, that conveniently out-of-sight target for funding cuts by overpaid London solipsists, always came into its own in a crisis. The predictable playlists; the cheesy chat; the interviews with desperate fading celebrities; the tired attempts at *fun*: all were forgiven when community cohesion was called for. Those presenters you normally couldn't/wouldn't listen to become your best friends, saviours, mates-in-arms against unforeseen misfortune. Disaster provided the opportunity to reconnect. Purpose was re-established.

A reporter Terry had known since before they were at school together was standing in front of the flooded roundabout, wind-shielded microphone in hand, facing the camera he'd set up on the gale-resistant tripod.

The scene took Terry back to the time he'd walked past the local court where – that rarest of events – a trial of national interest was being conducted. The entry road leading to the court building had been crammed with sumptuous news vans, engineers, make-up artists, lighting crews and the rest, all serving the delightfully coiffured on-air talent from the major national networks. And there, at the very back, this same local video journalist, alone with the camera. *Disproportionality.* The Word of the Day.

Today, Terry waited until the reporter finished his piece and raised his hand gingerly.

"Alright Stephen?" he said, approaching the man.

Stephen Irwin was tall, thick-set and tolerably good-looking in a granite-faced sort of way. At school, he'd been known as Amir due to his disconcerting habit of looking over your shoulder when talking to you to see if someone more important was behind.

"Ah'm 'ere," an irritated Michael Crane had once said, and the phrase had instantly been corrupted to 'Amir', a name generally unfamiliar in this monocultural outpost of the British Isles in the 1970s.

"Oh, hi Terry," he said. "Just doing a piece for the 6 o'clock telly."

"Are you still on the radio as well?" said Terry.

"Sometimes, but you've got to be responsive to today's multi-platforming needs in this game."

As his voice tailed off, his expression softened, almost imperceptibly.


*There it is*, thought Terry. *The eyes drifting away from my face. Stephen Irwin, Eternal Seeker of the Better Offer.*


How reassuring.

"This looks bad," said Terry, indicating the swirling waters.

"Yes. The experts are assessing it all now. They may have to rebuild that bridge carrying the road to Scotland if the foundations have been loosened."

"It sounds serious," said Terry. "We'd better not jump up and down or we could weaken the structure even more."

Stephen's eyes panned back to Terry's face and his voice switched to the Karloffian timbre he used on-air when relaying bad-news stories [*or sometimes with him,* thought Terry unkindly, *bad news stories*].

"This isn't a joking matter, Terry. In fact, I've just heard from the police that a cyclist is missing and may have drowned down at the Holmes. I'm heading there now."

Terry watched him lift his camera and walk away and thought, *he's as unhinged as ever, he's disconnected, his moods turn on a word, he has no sense of humour*. And remembered how – hard to credit it now in this shiny futuristic reality – when they were children living in adjacent streets, the ragman would roll by on his horse-drawn cart and the horse would open its bowels onto the road and Stephen Irwin would run out and cram the steaming yellow strawy mess into his welcoming pink infant mouth.

You reap what you sow.

**41**

Ernie.

Faithful, reliable Ernie rang the police from a *telephone box*, remember them? Odd to see one surviving on the corner of the road into the site: it's because of all the walkers doing the Wall.

Not today though.

"I was on the path along the Holmes just now and am sure I saw somebody get blown into the river just down from Jollyboys Hill. What? I was up on the top path. Yes, I ran down. There's a bike in the water but I couldn't see the rider. What? No, I don't want to give my name. 'Bye."

He got back in the car where Eric was shaking.

"Did you tell them?"

"Yes, Eric."

"I can't stand it Ernie. Carol's happily cutting hair at this very minute, not knowing what's coming her way. Drive me home. It's not too late."

"Yes, Eric. Whatever you want."

"But then he'll come for us. Mark Richardson. He'll hurt her to get at me. That's what he said. If I'm gone, she's safe."

Ernie waited silently. This was Eric's inner debate, to resolve on his own. The pair had talked it through again and again over the past weeks. Ernie had no more to give so now he said nothing. Through all the discussions, he wondered what he'd do in Eric's position. But then, he knew he'd never be in Eric's position. He'd have acted straight away. Perhaps people could smell decisiveness, latent power, whatever it was about him, so he wouldn't ever get to where Eric was now.

All those years ago, the start of secondary school, he was the only black kid in the place – possibly in the town – and, for the first few months, he was the whipping boy for every warped racist view held by the many meat-heads (teachers included) he encountered almost daily. When verbal taunts began to morph into physical threats, he started Karate classes and he was a natural.

100

Within weeks, his confidence grew, the bullying stopped, and he hadn't had to do a thing. Somehow, they sensed it, the meat-heads, not to mess with him anymore.

Eric, though. He wasn't the same. He wasn't a coward, but his life had been compromised by an over-cautious approach to challenge, a hedging of bets, an inbuilt aversion to risk. He acts, thought Ernie, but only *eventually*. Eric, thought Ernie, is like most people and I'm not.

"What do I *do*?" said Eric.

He got out of the car, coatless, into the wild rain, sky almost dark, wind vamping a cracked melody through bare creaking trees. Ernie felt the thuds of his fist on the roof, forceful then quickly ebbing and Eric got back in.

"I see it through," he said.

He was almost convincing.

This new normal, it soon became clear to Eric, was only survivable if you could maintain a sense of depersonalisation; become a stranger to yourself; a robot; remain in a dream.

The caravan site was within walking distance of two villages. The less interesting inland one had a pub with a small shop attached. He decided he would go to the pub to eat, aiming to make sure he chose busy times so that he wouldn't stand out. He quickly realised, though, that at this time of year there were no busy times but went anyway, hopeful but not convinced that his relationship with the mousy barmaid would never progress beyond the strictly functional.

"Do you want to see the menu? Today's Specials are on the board."

A sentence that seemed appropriate in this ghost town.

The shop provided him with the basics, but he'd need more very soon. He also worried constantly that his anonymity would quickly wear off. How long did he have before this would happen? Weeks? Or maybe only days? Essential to fade away before you became familiar.

Eric walked a lot following his disappearance, mainly in the early morning or the evening when he could melt into the darkness. By exercising to the point of exhaustion, he was just about able to stop his fears from overwhelming him. He constantly imagined the agonies Carol and his far-off children might be going through but did his best to avoid confronting them.

There wasn't a newsagent for four miles so he didn't see any billboards that might refer to him. Another part of his stress management was keeping his radio tuned only to national stations, where a missing persons story was unlikely to be picked up. Even so, he switched it off during news bulletins, just in case. Ernie, they'd agreed, wouldn't make contact until Eric rang him. Disturbing statistics intermittently emerged about loneliness and the number of (particularly older) people who went for days, weeks, months in silent isolation. Eric found it very easy to join their ranks.

During his second week of absence, Eric found himself in the nearby coastal village late one afternoon and saw a notice board beside the post-box. Amongst mainly out-of-date announcements about upcoming flower sales that had long since gone, or the previous summer's Bowling Club fixtures, or the minutes of the 'next' (but really two back) Parish Council meeting, was a card with a faded message scrawled on it:

**Scooter for sale. 50cc. Good condition. Suit learner. £150 ono.**

An address was written underneath.

He found the house and knocked on the door. Loud coughing came from inside then the door opened, and a grey face peered out at Eric.

"I've come about the scooter."

The grey face looked confused.

"It's up for sale. On the notice board."

"Ah put that card up two yeer ago," said the old, old man.

"Have you still got it? The scooter?" said Eric.

"Aye. Neebody wanted it roond ere. Thev aw got cars these days."

"Can I see it?"

To Eric's surprise, the scooter had been well maintained. The tyres were blown up, the petrol tank half-full and the engine fired first time.

"Can I buy it?" said Eric.

"Aye. Ah've lost ownership document though. Ye'll av te sort that oot. Ah'll knock ye fifty quid off fer the trouble an theer's a helmet."

Eric, with no intention of sorting out the ownership, rode the machine back to the site. In front of his caravan was a huge empty storage box for garden equipment. By twisting the handlebars sharply, the scooter could be made to sit snugly inside it, out of sight. There was a side entrance to the site near to his plot and he took to wheeling the scooter out of it before starting the engine. The place was empty and the security patrols still almost non-existent, but Eric was pathologically cautious these days.

With this added freedom to travel further afield, Eric was now able to mingle in some of the bigger towns down the West coast. He knew these places as stops on his old work route and, as he rode parallel to the railway line, he'd occasionally see a train whizzing past. Sometimes, he felt a yearning to buy a ticket and take a trip for old time's sake then he'd remember the day of the shouting, the lurching to a halt, the open door, the body down in the valley bottom… For Eric, despite his later court testimony, that was the day when he'd known for certain he was a coward.

He mustn't ever again go anywhere he couldn't melt into the background. This was his life now. His new reality.

**42**

Terry paid scant attention to the post-flood newspaper billboards Eric Bell was so keen not to see. He had already entered what his consultant later defined as *a protracted period of accelerative disengagement* from the world around him. An *emerging cognitive dissonance.*

Subtle changes began to impinge on his personality.

He was, for instance, no longer able to work with background music on. The twin activities of thinking and listening, both demanding his full attention, now cancelled each other out, leaving him in a state of mental inertia.

Watching television or cinema films also became almost impossible due to a nascent aversion to wasting time, this same impulse leading him to avoid meeting friends, colleagues, and acquaintances for trivialities such as morning coffee or an evening in the pub.

A related obsession with being productive made it ever-harder for him to relax: not until he'd done enough work, exercise, cleaning up, letter-writing, learning, *thinking* – his definition of 'enough' continually modifying to incorporate more and more activity – could he rest.

'*I'm on the road to madness,*' became his recurring internalised mantra.

Terry's life had begun to exist as a long series of balancing couplets, both lines sharing the same rhythm, tempo, number of syllables but with words that managed to be both similar and different. His divided perceptions rhymed with each other, but he no longer knew which, if any, was real life.

The shift that caused him the most concern was a terror – *terror* – that he was in real danger of losing (or, on the worst occasions, had already lost) his ability to filter what he was about to say as bizarre thoughts of unfathomable provenance swam into his head. Introduced to someone new, for example, he would have parallel phrases fighting for emersion from his mouth, one recognisably normal, the other a generally unacceptable alternative almost always containing a gratuitously offensive physical or sexual reference.

On one level, Terry saw this disjuncture as not uncommon; it was a standard device in TV comedies where the viewer was made aware that what the protagonist saw wasn't what they were thinking [*still frame of fire-breathing dragon as voiceover mentions mother-in-law*]. But it was the extremeness of his unacceptable alternatives which concerned him: the thought that he might be developing symptoms of dementia; the horror that, one day soon, the filters in his head would clog completely and the dark side would take over. The filters would clog. Completely.

His sense of detachment, of otherness, extended to places he knew. Again, he didn't think this unusual in itself. You were bound to associate what you saw today with how you'd seen the same physical space in the past. But Terry found this mash-up of *now* and *then* increasingly destabilising because it all seemed so real.

At its most acute, he could be walking down a familiar road, look up particular driveways and see those houses' former occupiers going about the business he'd historically known them to go about: old man Lamonby, long gone, now back pulling weeds from between the flagstones; Curly Hodgson, killed at 22, just disappearing into the back door with groceries for his mother; Nellie Hunter taking a tray of lemonade into the garden for the children and husband Dick.

Not ghosts but mirages created by his uncontainable imagination and memory, insubstantial holograms temporarily solid. He couldn't keep them away any more than he could view these historical fragments through a lens of nostalgia or sentimentalism. They weren't reassuring pictures from the past but uncomfortable eddies in the Sea of Time.

One memorable day, worlds collided when Terry saw a bikini-clad Sheila Williamson, 19, beautiful and knowing it, leaning against the front wall of 14 Well Bank Road just before her 62-year-old present self walked into view and caused the younger version to wink out of existence like a bursting bubble.

It was this mindset that would make his sighting of Eric Bell, two years hence, so vivid.

# 43

Eric made it until the end of January before he called Ernie again.

"How's Carol?" he said immediately. Like they were mid-conversation.

"Not great," said Ernie. "As you'd expect. Phases. Disbelief. Not accepting you've gone. Hoping you'll reappear at any minute. Sad. Tearful. Angry."

"Angry?" said Eric.

"With you, for being so stupid. 'Why would he go down there in that weather?' And with herself. 'I should have packed in work when he did then we'd have been together.' That kind of thing."

"How about the police?"

"Well, they had boats and frogmen out as soon as the wind died down. They put fishermen and landowners along the river on alert. But I think they've now decided you're really gone."

"So, what happens next?"

"Camilla's been to see Carol a lot, which makes me feel like a right swine. She's talking about moving, maybe away. She says it'll stop her going to the phone all the time."

"The phone?"

"Cammie says Carol can't go more than ten minutes without checking the landline, see if you've called and she missed it, or if you've left a message on the answerphone. Says Carol knows she's not being rational but can't help herself."

"Is she still at the hairdresser's?"

"She hasn't been back since the day you disappeared. As I say, she wants to keep checking the phone. Heartbreaking. Not sure what the money situation is for her."

"There's a life insurance policy."

"She said that to cash it in she'd have to get you declared dead and she can't. Not yet, Eric. Christ, she won't have a funeral for you."

Ernie answered Eric's other questions about the rest of the family and confirmed that the initial tiny flurry of media interest had petered out quickly.

"Those floods devastated the whole area. You were just one small part of an enormous disaster," was how Ernie put it.

Over the next couple of months, Eric rang Ernie only occasionally, refusing all his offers to drive out to the caravan park.

"I've got to hang on on my own for now," he said.

In truth, he wasn't sure what he was hanging on for as he'd already swept past the point of no return. [*Hadn't he?*] It was like he had jumped down a hole and the further he fell, the more he hoped to lose sight of what he was leaving behind. The problem was, it didn't seem to work out that way. His keen sense of Carol's suffering never left him, amplified by his feelings of guilt. He had to constantly remind himself of why he was doing all this; of Mark Richardson; of some far-off sense of justice for a dead girl who didn't care one way or the other what he had lost.

When March came, the site reopened for the new season and owners and visitors began to dribble back. Eric showed that he'd moved in by taking down the thick blackout curtains that had concealed him throughout the winter, replacing them with chintzy white voiles more typical of the park aesthetic.

Being situated on the more affordable non-resident side of the field, it wasn't too difficult to keep aloof from his transient and intermittent neighbours. He made sure he gave out enough friendly waves and greetings to counter any possible accusations of weirdness, but he aimed for and achieved 'friendly but private' status.

In April, Ernie told Eric he'd been declared dead, circumstances circumventing the usual seven-years-missing rule, and that Carol was moving away but not selling up. She wasn't saying where to. The house would be rented out. Despite the legal declaration, she continued to cling to her irrational hope (or instinct?) that her husband was still alive.

As May arrived though, it was no longer possible to put off Eric's funeral and the arrangements were made. Ernie relayed the details and Eric spent the morning he was being laid to rest riding the scooter up around the fells to take his mind off what he knew his family and friends would be going through.

In the afternoon, he rang Ernie to see how it had gone.

"Very dignified, Eric," said Ernie. "No coffin but a big photo of you on the altar in the cemetery chapel. People, the kids, Carol, said nice things about you.

*I* said nice things about you, which was peculiar. Carol kept it religion-free, just like you'd have wanted. We all joined Elvis in singing *The Wonder of You* at the end."

The days wove on: another winter, another year; Eric's capitulation to his undiminished desire to see his wife [now his *widow*]; trips to the seaside; the cemetery; the meeting with Brian Yeomans.

Bringing him (and us) to the end of Chapter 37 again:

*The more he thought about it, the less able he was to focus. He also knew that he was avoiding the big elephant in the room that was his head: what if Carol didn't want him back?*

*"I'll give it till Saturday and decide then," he told Ernie on the phone. "Don't let me put it off any longer than that."*

Saturday arrived.

# 44

Terry had been home from the hospital for 24 hours. He still had that little kick of extra energy which followed each revival from his attacks. Even Pat, a staunch realist, conceded that he looked well and displayed no obvious symptoms or lingering effects after the latest episode.

The birthday party the band had been rehearsing for was that night. Pat had contacted the other members after Terry's collapse and told them it was highly unlikely he'd be well enough to perform and they might want to cancel. Whether through inertia, laziness or pure optimism, though, nobody had done anything, so the gig was still scheduled to go ahead.

"They always bail on making decisions," said Terry. "How many times have we seen it? Good musicians but no initiative. Par for the course with creative people maybe? Anyway, it's worked in their favour this time."

"I can ring the organiser and explain," said Pat. "Say you've been in hospital and that's why I'm so late letting her know. Say you're not up to it."

"But I am up to it," said Terry. "Let's not let anybody down."

He went upstairs to sort out his equipment and write out the set lists as he knew no one else would. He'd been doing this for a long time now, lots of years, but he still expected something to go wrong.

Another *Where's Tim?* moment, perhaps?

Tim.

His band then, a different line-up just out of their teens with some chance of wider success after three years of regular local gigging. Versatile and adaptable. Terry, Vic and Tim. Vic Onslow, good drummer, solid individual and a professional. Tim Pickering, nice lad, excellent bass player but ulcer-inducingly unreliable. The unreliability factor upped when he met Sandra, young love, first love, yukkity-yuk.

Terry remembered the place: the Grove Restaurant. The owner's 50th birthday. He'd seen the band playing [*music, not soccer*] at the Football Club Valentine's Night Dance and booked them for his special event. The other side of the family would be travelling from Italy. Family is important to the Italians, thought Terry.

They dropped off the equipment in the morning, a rare luxury but it would ease the pressure later, and promised to be back at 6.30. It was raining that day, spring-into-summer rain, not quite refreshing but no longer stinging cold. Terry and Vic drew up the set lists over a lunchtime ice cream in the park cafe, the sounds of hissing coffee machines, meat sizzling and tables scraping accompanying the crucial ordering of numbers. Vic was the only other musician Terry had ever worked with who had an eye on everything that needed to be done. All the rest couldn't see beyond their own pleasure.

Like Tim.

Arriving at The Grove at the agreed time, Terry and Vic waited 10 minutes then went inside.

"It's gonna be a great party," said Guido, the owner.

"Plenty of dancing," said Miriam, Mrs Musetti.

They set up, sound checked as best they could then it was 7.15 and Tim still hadn't appeared.

"Your friend is late," said Mr Musetti.

"He's been at the dentist," said Vic, blushing.

"Start playing about 8?" said Miriam.

Those pre-mobile days.

Terry and Vic went outside.

"Where is he?" said Vic without enthusiasm and an underpinning despair borne of prior experience.

They went to Sandra's flat, five minutes' walk away. They heard noises. They knocked on the door. The noises stopped. Vic, about to shout Tim's name, saw the finger go to Terry's lips. They withdrew quietly. They went out of the front entrance hall, up the street, turned left and left again, walked down the back lane, and stood outside the locked yard door.

Toss a coin. Vic's hands dirty from whatever was on the bottom of Terry's shoes, hauling him up onto the shiny sloping roof of the outhouse. Terry, a step forward and a slip back, inching his way up to Sandra's window. Semi-darkness, an unnecessary fire in the grate, the yellow flames licking across Tim's bare-nekkid bouncing buttocks, Sandra's airborne ankles. Terry, edging back down the wet slates.

"I think we can forget about Tim."

Back to the Grove to explain that the bass-player's been involved in a collision.

"He set off driving before the anaesthetic wore off," said Vic.

"We'll do our best with just drums and guitar," said Terry.

It was almost a success but there was no ridding the room of the taint of disappointment.

"Thank you, boys," says Guido, wallet in hand. "I hope your other member recovers from his injuries soon."

"We can't take any money," said Terry and Vic in almost the same words at the same moment.

Packing the equipment into the car, Miriam appeared.

"You let Guido down," she said without recrimination.

She turned and went back in. Everything was in the car except Tim's bass and amplifier. They drove off into the night, pausing only to jam the scribbled-on beer mat through Sandra's letterbox.

"Thanks Tim. Left your equipment at the Grove for you to pick up tomorrow."

They decided not to tell him he'd been in an accident.

# 45

The two were back outside Brian Yeomans's house for Eric's Day of Reckoning. Ernie made small talk on the journey in, deliberately leaving space for Eric to run and rerun his decision about Mark Richardson.

"Ernie. Eric," said Brian, shaking their hands in turn. He again showed them into the lounge, where each took the same seats as before.

"Three coffees and a plate of biscuits," he shouted into thin air.

"Right," came the indistinct reply from an unidentifiable location.

Eric had already resumed combing his hand through his hair and was starting to perspire. His eyelids drooped, as if closing off the outside world would save him having to declare his decision. The others waited patiently until he was ready.

"I…," he began but was interrupted by a clattering as the half-opened door swung back and the youth on whose fingers Ernie had performed baseball bat surgery appeared, a large wooden tray in his hands. He placed the tray on the small table and turned to leave but Brian Yeomans coughed, and he stopped and looked at his grandfather, an expression of reluctant defiance on his face.

"Have you forgotten what you were going to say?" said Brian.

"No. Well…I mean, I'm…"

"Spit it out," said Brian.

The youth pulled back his shoulders and moved his legs slightly apart, like a private on parade. As he clasped his hands in front of him, Ernie caught a glimpse of the still-bandaged fingers.

"I apologise," he slowly began, directing his gaze at Ernie. "I'm sorry for threatening you. I didn't realise…"

As his voice tailed into nothing, Brian jumped in.

"He didn't realise what a sad twat he was trying to shake down old people, did you Shane?"

Shane's face went bright crimson.

"Christ, Shane," said Ernie. "You mean, after you had a go at me, you threatened somebody *old* as well?"

The teenager began rocking on his heels, unsure of the next move.

"OK Shane," said Brian. "Fuck off home."

As he moved back towards the door, Ernie stood up.

"Shane," he said. "A pro always picks on somebody his own size. At least then, even if you get the shit kicked out of you, you hang on to a bit of dignity. Self-respect. Think about it."

The boy sloped out. Ernie sat down again, and he and Brian looked at Eric, still lost in his own head.

"Brian," he said at last. "I appreciate your offer to fix my problem, but I can't let you. I've given it a lot of thought, but I can't let you. Ask you. If somebody's going to sort out Mark Richardson, it must be me. Thanks, but I have to face up to him. Them. The family."

"Eric," said Ernie.

"A word please, Ernie," said Brian Yeomans quickly and the pair stepped into the hallway.

When they came back in, Eric was on his feet.

"I mean, thanks again Brian but that's my decision."

"Fair enough," said Brian Yeomans, taking Eric's outstretched hand. "If you change your mind, let me know. Good luck."

When they went back out onto the drive, wisps of snow were drifting down onto the cold ground. As the car reached the corner of the road, they spotted Shane Yeomans hurrying along, his short denim jacket pulled tight against his scrawny frame. Ernie slowed and let down the nearside window.

"Do you want a lift, boy?" he shouted.

"No…" Shane stammered. "But…but…thanks for asking."

**46**

Terry's equipment and stage clothes, checked and quadruple-checked, were loaded and ready to go. He had two hours to kill before setting off so made a sandwich and sat at the kitchen window, watching the white flakes falling outside. Pat had gone to see the neighbours about upcoming dog-feeding duties and Terry took advantage of the time alone to try to relax and clear his head.

He washed his plate and mug and contemplated the unopened Christmas cards piling up on the bookcase. They never opened their cards until Christmas Eve because by then it was too late to send any to people they'd forgotten. The theory was that anyone they'd forgotten wasn't someone they wanted to send a card to, but it didn't always work out that way.

Shuffling idly through the envelopes, he caught the familiar faded scent clinging to one but couldn't quite retrieve the memory that would tell him whose it was. He wafted the letter up and down in some hopeless *aide-memoire* gesture. Scanning the handwriting on the fronts of the cards, he knew that Pat would recognise each of the senders but his abilities in grasping details like that rested in other areas.

Dropping the cards, he heard the tiny scratching at the kitchen door that heralded the arrival of the cat. Pulling the door open, he observed a rare reversal in the world order as the cat ran in followed by a mouse, he'd presumably been carrying but had dropped.

"No!" said Terry to the rodent. "Turn round. Get out while you can."

The mouse seemed to understand and made a swift exit. As the cat, realising his lapse, turned to follow, Terry pushed the door closed just in time. The thwarted creature hissed malevolently for a second then, with impressive nonchalance, forgot about his prey and began mopping up the meaty mess slopped into his bowl.

Terry wandered over to the stereo, once again thanking his non-present, superseded alternate selves for resisting the temptation to throw out or sell his records during the now-reversed vinyl purge of the CD Years.

He flicked through the narrow box of LPs – there were many more in the loft, but his favourites had barely changed since his first purchase at the age of 11 – and picked out *Hot Hits 5*. It was one of the umpteen budget-label collections of cover versions of 'current chart hits' released throughout the 1970s bearing the actual or implied challenge,

*Can you tell the difference between these and the original recordings?*

The question always made him smile because he now considered that these *were* the original recordings, a lasting testament to the days when money was tight and 12 'hits' (in whatever form) for 71p were preferable to just one (and a usually duff B-side) on a 50p single.

The same manufacturing mindset had led to those plastic toys found in seaside novelty shops of the same era featuring the likes of *Searay*, *Catman*, *Thunderwings*, *Capt. Crimson* and *Dr?* – not exactly the real thing but close enough then and now, somehow, *more* authentic. An alternative truth.

The sleeve of *Hot Hits 5* showed a lustrously haired girl in <u>hot pants</u> [now an almost illegal term in the febrile, censorious present] dancing against an exotic, shadowy, deep green backdrop. As with the session artists within, she wasn't foregrounded as a real model [*and where is she now? her and her grandchildren?*] because her name wasn't mentioned on the sleeve credits. (Though later volumes did give names, Terry seemed to recall. Why?)

Partway through the first track, *Knock Three Times*, he wondered for the umpteenth time if he preferred the cover versions because of the lack of baggage they carried. You didn't have to wonder what happened to the performers because you didn't know who they were in the first place. Never had. It didn't matter. Unlike the real stars of the time [*all of whom will eventually fade to the same nothingness, albeit at different speeds*] with their subsequently publicised personal turbulations, these performers were fixed in anonymous immortality. The song was the thing.

Almost ready to leave, Terry made a stress-induced lavatory visit first. One hand pressing on the tiles above the cistern, he watched the golden stream [*once the name of a quickly-rebranded-for-the-UK Chinese tea*] course into the toilet bowl.

*It smells like the effluence of an old man,* he thought.

No point denying a truth you only share with yourself.

When he arrived at the venue, Martin and Gary were already there.

"What kept you?" said Martin sardonically.

"I was plastering some walls," said Terry, not in any mood for banter.

Following the sound check, Gary, who lived five minutes away and was notoriously bad at filling the empty hour until the band's first set, wanted to go home for a cup of tea [*Golden Stream?*].

"I'll stay here and keep an eye on the gear," said Terry.

"Do you want me to stop as well?" said Martin, his intonation leaving no doubts as to his inclination.

"No, you're OK," said Terry. "But could you both just sort out the set-lists before you go off?"

He knew they wouldn't.

They left Terry sitting in the club, empty save for the two bar-staff down at the other end of the room. It was these quiet periods of contemplation before and after a gig that he loved. About 10 minutes later, a mature woman in a black sparkly dress and red high heels walked in and looked round. The bar-staff had disappeared, so she approached Terry.

"Excuse me," she said. "Are you the manager?"

He stood up.

"No. I'm in the band."

"Oh, hello," she said. "Was it you I spoke to when I booked you?"

It had to be because, in 15 years of playing together, neither Martin nor Gary had ever negotiated a booking. *It's your band*, they always said, cleverly managing to celebrate their own idleness whilst implicitly criticising his industry.

"Yes," he said. "I'm Terry. You must be Jill. Happy birthday."

"Thanks," she said. "Pleased to meet you. I am and it's not till tomorrow but thanks."

She had a carrier-bag in her hand with three rolls of paper sticking out of the top.

"The club said I could pin these up but I'm not sure where. Don't want to cause any damage."

"One of the bar-staff's come back," said Terry. "He'll know."

She tottered off and Terry sat down to write out the set lists before the arrival of the first customer. Her paper-hanging activity became a white noise as he wrestled with the choices that would help determine whether the evening would flow with energy and excitement.

"Does that look straight?"

He glanced up. She'd pinned on the wall a poster-size photograph of herself and a man at what looked like another party and taken, he guessed, maybe a dozen years ago.

"It's fine," said Terry.

There was a pregnant pause.

"It's my husband and me," said Jill. "At my 50$^{th}$, ten years ago."

Terry could feel the subliminal urging within her spoken words. She wanted him to ask about the husband. He resisted momentarily, knowing it wouldn't be good news, but he was incapable of sustained churlishness. And it was her birthday.

"You haven't changed a bit," he said, then, "Is he coming along later?"

"No," she said flatly. "He's not."

She turned, the urging gone and a new leadenness in her gait. Terry watched her walk away.

*Another story*, he thought. *So many stories.*

**47**

Now Eric Bell was double thinking. As Ernie once again drove him back out to the caravan he was considering how, by saying he'd deal with Mark Richardson, he'd maintained some personal integrity. Alongside this thought, however, sat the possibility that he was a complete idiot. What could he do against a certifiable thug and his very dangerous family? *Complete idiot* was winning the internal debate.

"Why am I so stupid?" he said as they approached the site, his first words since they'd left Brian Yeomans's house.

"You're not stupid," said Ernie. "You're conflicted. It's obvious and it's allowed."

"But how could I ever hope to take on Mark Richardson and come out alive?"

"It could be done," said Ernie. "If you were willing to forget the rules. Be cunning."

"How do you mean?"

"The thing about most people is they've got this weird sense of honour. Think they should play fair. Give their enemies a fighting chance. That's OK if you're up against somebody following the same code but you can't meet Richardson and his like on those terms."

Eric blinked, still uncomprehending.

"Let me tell you about when I first learned this," said Ernie, stopping the car.

Ernie was in the last-ever intake at the boys' secondary modern. The following year, it would amalgamate with the girls' school down the road but, for now, the opposite sex (for there were still only two then) was off the radar.

They'd been warned in the last year at junior school to prepare for the trauma that would occur as they went from small school top of the heap to big school bottom but, probably fortunately, most people got through the summer without contemplating the potential horrors ahead.

When Ernie and the other six boys from his old class turned up for their first day at the new school, the main difference they all noticed straight away was the

118

increase in noise levels. Childish enthusiasm would henceforth begin its uneasy transition into adolescent loudness.

"How was your first day?" said Ernie's dad that evening.

"OK, except everybody shouts all the time," said Ernie.

The other big change to get used to was understanding territorial and temporal boundaries, particularly during morning and lunch breaks. From having free rein to play where they wanted in the juniors, Ernie and the rest now had to learn a complex series of rules relating to when and where they could and couldn't go. To get anything wrong was to incur the wrath of the older boys who, having experienced it themselves, felt duty-bound to make the new intake suffer as much as was invisibly possible.

The football pitch was where dominion was most keenly contested, the pecking-order most firmly established. The top half of the field was for the exclusive use of the third-years (all older students having separate facilities). The bottom half was used by first-years on the understanding that second-years were entitled to usurp them at any time or – an even less welcome alternative – join in with the game.

Inevitably, there were always boys in the second year it was particularly advisable to avoid. In Ernie's case, David Johnston and Melvyn Rourke quickly became well-known for their sadistic bullying of the new arrivals. Their technique was to interrupt a peaceful first-year game by running on the pitch and kicking the ball as far away as they could. They would then, *a la* Rusty Davis, point at someone and tell him to go and collect it. When he brought it back, they'd kick it away again and repeat the humiliation.

Ernie was picked out during a mid-morning kick-about in the third week. As the ball sailed into the distance, Rourke pointed at him and said,

"Go and get it and hurry up."

Ernie didn't give himself time to think.

"Go and get it yourself," he said.

Rourke walked over to him, punched him square on the jaw then walked away, ordering another boy to collect the ball. Ernie almost fainted with the pain.

At the end of break, he shuffled back into school with tears streaming down his face. On the landing of the stairs leading to his classroom stood the headteacher. Ernie stopped in front of her.

"Melvyn Rourke hit me, miss. I think he's broken my jaw."

She looked at him with what he later realised was pure contempt.

"Grow up and get to your class," she said sharply.

It was Ernie's first real experience of injustice and it pained him as much as his dislocated jaw.

That night, Ernie's dad once again asked how his day had been.

"OK," said Ernie.

"Is something wrong with your mouth?"

"I got knocked going upstairs. My face hit the wall."

Ernie avoided football after that. At first, he was worried Melvyn Rourke might seek him out and hit him again then he realised that he wasn't significant. He was just another casualty in a long line of ongoing, instantly forgotten victims. The pain in his face lessened but his desire for vengeance grew.

He took to observing Rourke's movements outside the classroom and discovered that he went to school rugby practice straight after the home bell on Tuesday afternoons. His need for revenge fuelling his obsession, Ernie noted that, when rugby practice ended at 4.00 p.m., Rourke walked most of the way home with two other boys. However, the others peeled off two streets before Rourke's house and he always finished the journey alone.

The houses along one of the streets were interrupted by the wall of a disused yard halfway along. It was behind this wall one Tuesday that Ernie stood on an abandoned chair and waited. As Melvyn Rourke walked past, Ernie dropped the breezeblock he'd found in the yard straight onto his head. Rourke fell forward with an agonised cry then there was silence. Peering over the top of the wall, Ernie saw him lying motionless. Quickly clambering down onto the pavement, Ernie ran off down the street.

"He didn't come back to school for about three weeks," said Ernie. "The word was he had a fractured skull, but nobody knew for sure."

"How did you feel about hurting him?" said Eric.

"That was the thing," said Ernie. "I realised I was pleased. He deserved it. My only regret was not letting the headteacher have it as well for doing nothing about the bullying."

"Did Rourke ever find out it was you?"

"No. How could he?"

"Did he stop being a bully?"

"No," said Ernie. "He carried on and I gave up the break-time soccer."

"So, he won," said Eric.

"I didn't care about the football," said Ernie. "If I had, I'd have gone after him again. No, he didn't win."

Eric wasn't sure what to make of it.

"The point of the story is this," said Ernie. "Can you definitely see yourself dealing with Mark Richardson without mercy and without him knowing it's you?"

Eric's hand went up and through his hair yet again as he considered the question. He didn't know and Ernie knew he didn't know.

"'If an injury has to be done to a man it should be so severe that his vengeance need not be feared.'"

"What?" said Eric.

"Machiavelli. It's something I heard once and remembered. It's got to be all or nothing."

Eric Bell saw his own face, uncertainty etched across it, reflected in the darkened car window.

"Eric," said Ernie. "It's not you. Is it?"

Eric's head bobbed slowly around like the vehicle's back-shelf toy dog.

**48**

Martin and Gary came back with five minutes to spare and no set lists.

"We'll use the one from the last gig," said Martin.

"Have you got it with you?" said Terry.

"No," said Martin after some half-hearted scrabbling through a small stack of papers.

"I might have one," said Gary, but he hadn't.

Terry handed out the three copies of the new one he'd prepared.

"See, I told you he'd do it," said Martin triumphantly.

That was the moment Terry realised he'd finally and irreversibly had enough, but he gritted his teeth. As he strapped on his guitar, he investigated the heart of the now crowded room and saw Jill the Birthday Girl. She was surrounded by smiling happy friends but, despite the laughter, she seemed utterly and completely alone.

People were in celebratory mood from the start so the usual longueur before anyone danced was avoided until, midway through the fifth song, the bass stopped. Terry looked at Gary who was bent over his instrument, plugging it into an electronic tuner. Terry tried to carry on, but Martin stopped drumming and proceedings ground to an unexpected halt.

"Talk to them for five minutes," said Gary. "I've gone out of tune."

"Nobody noticed," said Terry. "Let's bash on. We'll lose them otherwise."

But Gary ignored him.

*I'm trapped*, thought Terry. *How many times has this happened? Or how many times have we been about to start a song when Martin asks me how it goes? We're amateurs. This is shabby. I'M NOT LIKE THIS. THEM.*

Terry ad-libbed for thirty seconds but no one was listening. He looked back again. Gary, still fiddling. Martin, *looking at his phone*. People starting to sit down. He moved to the mixer and picked up the mp3 player he'd dumped the between-sets background music onto.

"Sorry about the technical problems," he said into the microphone. "We'll be back as soon as we can."

Groans. Catcalls. The smell of defeat.

<h1 align="center">49</h1>

Not five miles away, at the same time. Now in the caravan, the spiralling repetitive self-recriminations. Again.

"You're right," said Eric Bell. "I haven't got the bottle. I've been useless all my life."

"Wallow in self-pity if you want," said Ernie, "but don't expect me to join in."

"I screwed up. With Brian Yeomans. He, you, gave me a chance and I bottled."

Ernie stood up.

"I'd better be getting home."

Eric, knowing he wouldn't sleep that night, this could be the start of his final decline, stupid to turn down the offer, you don't employ a joiner if you want some brain surgery done, you get a brain surgeon, *I'm the joiner and I've missed getting the brain surgeon*, that once-in-a-lifetime chance has gone. The thirty-million-pound lottery ticket. Thrown down the drain.

"Thanks Ernie," said Eric.

Ernie put out his arms. Eric was confused. Ernie wasn't a man who made physical gestures. Neither was Eric. Ernie flicked his fingers in invitation. Eric stood up between Ernie's arms. Ernie's arms folded around Eric's heaving body, his mouth pressing close to Eric's pulsating neck.

"Eric," said Ernie. "Not being a murderer doesn't make you useless. It's all set up. Brian's onto it. Mark Richardson will be dealt with."

# 50

Terry's best friend at primary school, Ian, knew a boy called Stuart Horseman. He was the only person in their social circle who lived in a house *all on its own* with a garage and a garden with trees in it. Moreover, Stuart's dad wore a suit and tie to work. [*"Not a shirt, though,"* joked Ian.]

There was a summer when Terry spent the whole of nearly every day in the Horseman garden, playing *Batman* with Ian and Stuart. Terry was Robin in a near-enough costume made by his mother. Ian was The Joker, in normal clothes but with who-knows-where-it-came-from? white make-up and red lipstick. Stuart was Batman in a perfect Bat-costume, exactly like Adam West's. Terry and Stuart hung upside down from the biggest tree, legs curled tight around the solid knotty branches until The Joker squirted them with his water-pistol and they Bat-dropped and Bat-ran after him through the Bat-bushes.

Terry realised, without being able to pin down why, that Stuart Horseman was different to other children he knew. He was generous, always handing out sweets and Jubbly orange drinks and never expecting anything back except a thank-you. He had parents who, like Stuart himself, always spoke quietly and used unfamiliar but interesting words. And Stuart looked different, his blond hair and aquiline nose giving him what Terry would now call an aristocratic air.

Shortly after that glorious Bat-summer, the Horsemans moved out of their house.

"They've gone to live in the country," said Ian.

"Which country?" said eight-year-old Terry.

"Africa," joked his geographically illiterate friend. [*typical Bat-villain*]

For months after, Terry would walk past that house all on its own and look at the Bat-tree and wonder how Stuart and his parents were managing in the heat down near the Equator.

Maybe six, seven years ago, Terry's mother asked him if he remembered Bat-Stuart Horseman and Terry nodded. She then told Terry of how Stuart Horseman, now a grown-up barrister and not back from Africa because he'd never moved there, had been out for an evening meal with his wife in a hotel just over the border in Scotland. As they were eating, a fight started at the bar between a local man and three men from Terry's hometown. When the three men attacked the local man, Stuart Horseman had gone across to intervene…

["Still the superhero," Terry said prematurely.]

…and the three had turned on Stuart and pushed him to the ground. It was never established who administered the mortal kick to the head.

Terry, now, at the party.

Waiting to start the second set, Gary and Martin were at the buffet when the distinguished older woman with the half-empty plate sat down beside him.

"Aren't you eating?" she said.

"I can't when I'm working," said Terry.

"You were awfully good," she said. "Despite that unfortunate break in the middle."

Terry nodded gracefully at the compliment.

"The bass player gets a little nervous," he said diplomatically.

"My daughter-in-law thinks you were excellent too."

She pointed at one of the posters.

"Ah, Jill's your daughter-in-law," he said.

"Yes. That's her with my son at her 50$^{th}$ birthday party."

"She told me," said Terry. "He looks like a nice man."

"Yes, he was," she said then, abruptly, tears starting. "I'll leave you in peace. I'm Melanie. Melanie Horseman. Lovely to meet you."

*What now?* thought Terry as Martin and Gary returned.

"Instead of concentrating on the 99% that's good, you always find the 1% bad." (Martin)

"So *you* say." (Gary)

"You suck all the joy out of it." (Martin)

Terry didn't know what they were talking about, nor did he care. He was like a slowly uncoiling spring, progressively unable or unwilling (he didn't know which) to rise to conflict. He wondered if his adrenal glands were malfunctioning but couldn't be sure as he didn't know what they did. Like so much of his current mental activity, it was an abstruse thought, its origin unclear. [*is that pleonastic?*].

The second set fell apart near the end. Martin counted in, Terry hit a **G** and Gary shouted out instead of playing the bassline. They stopped and Terry looked at Gary.

"It's in **A**," said Gary.

"It was too high for me to sing so we put it down a tone. Remember?"

"We rehearsed it in **A**."

"You can play it in **G** just as easily."

"We rehearsed it in **A**."

The exchange took perhaps ten seconds but when Terry turned to face the crowd again, the floor had almost completely cleared. They limped through the number, Terry gave a half-hearted,

"We'll be back shortly."

and they retreated to the small changing room behind the stage.

"I think we can call it a night at that," said Terry.

"But we haven't said a proper goodbye," said Gary.

"We've got to go back on," said Martin. "It would be unprofessional not to."

Terry was exhausted when he had expected to be exhilarated. He said nothing and examined the back of his left hand. A long red mock-vein ran down it to his wrist. It was where the cat had scratched him that morning. Maybe he had feline aphasia that periodically shut down his ability to communicate? His whimsies were curtailed by a head round the changing-room door.

"Hello lads," said the head. "Sorry to bother you but I thought that was great and wondered if you'd be interested in a gig."

Martin and Gary looked up expectantly.

"It's not till May next year. I run a little festival every year in aid of childhood cancer."

"How much?" said Martin.

"What?"

"Will you pay us?"

"It's for childhood cancer. Everybody works for nothing."

"Not me," said Martin. "You can take your fucking free work and stuff it up your fucking do-gooding arse…"

And on and on it went then stopped and Terry said,

"Me'n'Gary'll do it, won't we Gary?"

Gary looked uncertain.

"We'll use a stand-in drummer," said Terry, his voice even and toneless.

He wrote his number on a corner of the set-list, tore it off and passed it over.

"Thanks," said the head. "I'll be in touch."

The head exited and Terry stood up. He walked onto the stage. The crowd was strewn across the furniture, talking, or singing along to Terry's background music selection. There'd be no more dancing tonight, he knew. It was mellow-down time.

As he began to pack away his equipment, Jill Horseman appeared behind him.

"We've all had a great time," she said. "Thank you ever so much."

She handed him a brown sealed envelope. He opened it and counted the notes inside. He put two-thirds of them back in the envelope and handed the rest to her.

"No," she said. "It's for you. You worked for it."

"Sometimes," he said, seeing again Signor Musetti, "I meet people who are so nice, I'd rather not take their money. Happy birthday."

Spontaneously, she began to sob. Terry squeezed her shoulder and resumed his dismantling, thinking of the boy hanging in the tree beside him, the sweets and orange juice, the hot endless summer, the country of Africa, the space between his thoughts and the toecap colliding with bone, bone splintering into pink brain, shutdown, gone, forever gone.

Martin and Gary appeared.

"We haven't said goodnight," said Martin. "What are you doing?"

"Goodnight," said Terry. "I'm done. Tired. Weary."

"You f…"

And he was off again, Terry replacing teenage cancer festivals as the object of his fulminations. At the end of the diatribe, Terry took out the brown envelope and handed it to Martin.

"For you and Gary," he said.

"Have you taken your share?" said Gary.

Terry ignored the question, and no one repeated it. That said something but he wasn't yet sure what.

Later, Martin apologised but Terry felt nothing about any of it.

"It's the festival organiser you should apologise to," he said.

Martin, to his credit, went to find him while Terry and Gary finished loading the equipment.

"A simple 'no' would have been enough," said Gary. "Why did he have to go off on one like that? That was a nice guy asking us. He liked us. I'm not sure we could do that gig with a different drummer though."

The acceptable face of equivocation.

When Martin didn't reappear, Gary shook Terry's hand and wished him a Happy Christmas. Terry felt a warm wave of affection break over him.

"Keep in touch," said Gary.

He got in his car and started the engine. Just before he pulled away, he wound down the window.

"It's that house of Martin's," he said. "Too many things wrong with it. He's bitten off more than he can chew. It's sending him mad."

# 51

Eric Bell sat in his caravan and thought of unmanned drones. He'd seen footage of them on TV, guided towards their target by someone behind a computer screen thousands of miles away. There was always a moment in the news reports where you saw the destination – usually a street full of innocent civilians – in its normal state. Birdseye views of buildings, vehicles, yellow roads, people; many different people, none suspecting the next development, the bomb getting smaller as it drops from beneath the onboard camera. The silent explosion. The smoke. The flying bits. Parts. The quick pre-aftermath edits to spare the audience at home's feelings, poor sensitive souls, exposed to horror, there is an off-switch on that screen. Wasn't that a leg flying upwards? Let's watch it again in slow-motion.

Eric, in his dark lounge on a December Saturday night, was the drone driver [*pilot? even though not on board the aircraft? we need to rethink the meanings of some words*], Mark Richardson the dusty, unsuspecting, yellow-roaded street. Eric, a willing passenger on an unstoppable train – always a train? He still wasn't sure. Responsibility had been snatched from him, not he abdicating it; was that right?

Mark Richardson, one of three men seen but never identified at the vicious killing of highly regarded legal expert, Stuart Horseman, specialist subject: **human rights**. Eric Bell, not knowing this. Would it have made any difference if he did?

When would the bomb drop? Better not to know.

Eric looked again at the letter. Note. That Ernie had brought from the house. Hello Eric?

The same words he'd heard before the lawnmower box hit him on that long-off day…

# 52

Monday morning, Terry was back at the hospital, waiting down in the basement. The Psychology Department. It felt appropriate that all the seeable, findable ailments – limb fractures, head wounds, eyes, ears, *being old*, noses, throats, hernias, teeth, tumours, genetic discords, pregnancies [*an ailment?*], weeping leg sores – were dealt with on the ground and upper floors. The unseen, on the other hand – the in-your-head, you might be screwy, PTSD, therapy, *it's me nerves*, kind of business – was dealt with belowstairs. Fittingly [*don't mention fits to me*] hidden and out of sight [if not *outasight!*].

Terry sat on the sticky green chair and looked at the door in the recess on the opposite side of the corridor. The name-free, slide-along sign said

**ENGAGED**

Just like a telephone. Or a private eye. ['that's ophthalmics and private is twenty quid a go.'] But never married.

He waited. His appointment time passed by. At 47 minutes late, the door opened and a middle-aged woman with all the signs of being well-off, high-maintenance and over-enamoured of a glass or two of wine came out. *Wonder what's up with her*, thought Terry before she stopped in front of him and looked at a notepad in her hand.

"Are you Terry Ellis?" she said, reading from the pad.

"I am," said Terry.

"Sorry for the wait. Please come in."

He followed her into the empty room. There was an overwhelming smell of artificial raspberry in the air and the *Au Naturel* spray-mist bottle sat alone on the windowsill. She picked up a brown file from her desk, opened it and skimmed the top page.

"I'm Elspeth," she said when she'd finished reading. "Neurology asked me to see you. I understand you've been experiencing blackouts. Is that right?"

"Why have I been waiting?" said Terry.

"I'm sorry," said Elspeth.

"That's twice you've been sorry in three minutes. Once for being late and once because you don't know how to answer my question."

She turned bright crimson.

"I had some writing-up to do," she said.

"And I have work to go to," said Terry.

"Are you always confrontational?" she said.

"Are you always defensive?" he said. "Is quietly asking you why you've wasted 47 minutes of my time 'confrontational'?"

She looked at him with the expression of someone not used to being questioned. *Ironic, in her line of work*, thought Terry, but he'd seen it too often in his own job, this '*I'm doing you a favour just by being here*' attitude.

It reminded him of the film-star on the $12million fee who asked the director what his motivation was for the opening scene. "*$12million*," was the reply.

Her assumed superiority was, he realised, just another of the things he'd had enough of.

"Perhaps we should start again," she said.

"It's too late for that," said Terry. "Perhaps we should just start from here. After all, I don't want to wait another 47 minutes."

"What is your problem?" she said.

"Isn't that why I'm here?" he said. "For you to tell me."


*The trouble with this mind-games caper*, thought Terry, *is that its success hinges on my believing in it. Like religion. But I'm an atheist.*


Elspeth pressed on, asking her questions: how do you feel when you wake up in the morning? [*disconnected*]; is your job stressful? [*it's harder than yours*]; how's your relationship with your wife? [*good, how's yours with your husband or wife or partner?*]; have you ever felt like harming yourself? [**not till I came here today**].

It wasn't going to work. Terry could see through it, this phoney interrogation.

"Did you have a happy childhood?"

"Sorry Elspeth but I've been playing BS Bingo in my head and that question was the one that got me a full house. I'm here because I keep fainting or losing touch with the world around me, not because I want to sleep with my mother."

She would, she said, arrange for someone else to see him as this wasn't going anywhere.

"That's your conclusion?" said Terry. "How much are you on an hour?"

"That's my…"

"I pay your wages."

He left, feeling he'd known her a long time. She had all Linda's mannerisms, gestures, *look*. Linda, from whom he'd inherited his office and job all those years ago. Though she'd preferred her air fresheners to be lemon scented.

The day he started; it was obvious that the previous occupant (*La-La-La-La-La-La-Lay-Linda*) had made a hasty departure. The desk was strewn with papers and that type of stationery equipment it seems wasteful to throw out, but which isn't really worth keeping.

On the walls were the remnants of reminders to do now-irrelevant things: sticky notes; pinned pieces of paper; a calendar that hadn't been turned in three months; a whiteboard with half-erased messages; and an odd hand-drawn picture of someone's head with the crosshairs of a rifle-sight superimposed.

When he opened the desk drawers, empty bottles had rolled down two of them and bounced against the wooden fronts. There was a strong smell of lemon, and, in the top drawer, a number of letters bundled together and held by a petrifying rubber band.

Terry cleared the contents of the wall, desktop, and the bottles into the rusty-bottomed waste-bin but he didn't know what to do with the letters.

"They were just left in my desk drawers," he said to Pat that night. "I'm not sure if I should throw them out, read them or give them to somebody else to deal with."

"Unless you read them, you won't know if they're worth keeping or not," said Pat. "There might be something juicy in there."

"Then it's almost my duty to scrutinise them."

Next morning, he pulled out the bundle. As he did so, the petrified rubber snapped, and the letters scattered across the floor. He gathered them up and began reading the top one. It was to Linda from Brendan.

My darling,

it began [*Terry winced*]

I know we said we would sit down with Kay and tell her about us, but this isn't the right time. She has just been diagnosed with dyslexia.

As you might imagine, this has devastated her as she was hoping to be promoted and will now have to declare her condition to her manager. There is no reason why you and I can't continue to see each other but, for now, well I know you'll understand. That's why I love you.

Ever yours,
Brendan x


He spent his lunchbreak reading the rest, inspecting the envelopes, smelling the paper, speculating on whether the ink-runs were spilt alcohol or dropped tears... Brendan was a heel and Linda was being taken for a fool, probably willingly.

A couple of days later, Terry still hadn't decided what to do with them when he was visited by Linda.

"I'm your predecessor in this office," she said, sweeping in without knocking. "Linda Owens. I think I left some personal items in the desk drawers. I'll just take a quick look."

"Is that a request or an order?" said Terry.

The imperious look she gave him had been the same as the one he'd recently received from Elspeth the therapist. They shared the same arrogant confidence and expensive clothes.

"A request of course," she said, putting her hand on the top-drawer knob.

"Request denied," Terry said. "I have my own personal items in there now."

She looked at him, incandescent with anger.

"How dare you," she said. "They're my things. Do you really want me to go and see your manager?"

"If you think it'll get you anywhere, yes, go and ask him if you can rifle through my desk. I'm sure he'll be only too pleased to decide. Brendan's very good at making decisions, isn't he?"

She had turned and fled almost before he'd re-opened his eye after the wink.

When Terry left Elspeth's interrogation room, he went straight up to Neurology to seek out Jane Shepherd. He had to wait an hour before she returned. He explained what had happened in their meeting.

"I'm very grateful to you for trying to get me help," he said, "but that lady, Elspeth..."

He stopped talking.

His hands began to shake.

He held his arms out and they were trembling.

He could feel his eyes trying to burrow backwards into his brain.

His head started to flip-flop from side to side.

The consultant's door was rattling and began to open.

Terry, lurching to his feet, put both hands on the brass handle and tried to stop it turning but he could feel his strength diminishing.

Someone was behind him, pushing him out of the room through the widening gap. Four hands now, moving his contorting body slowly forward. They were there, in the corridor, the inky black corridor, the fused-lights corridor with the new staircase at the end. It hadn't been there when he arrived but now, he was climbing the stairs, creaking,

*I'm on my way, Claire. No need to push me, Mimi.*

DON'T PUSH!

# 53

Eric Bell could hear the dogs. They were howling in sheds just outside the caravan site. He'd rung the RSPCA on three occasions but, when he hadn't been able to confirm a 'visual sighting' (*what other kind of sighting is there?* Eric wondered), he'd been told there was nothing they could do.

Christmas was just over a week away, but Eric had barely thought about it. All he could think about was Carol, down there by the sea. What if, by some process beyond human understanding, Mark Richardson now knew that Eric had given the go-ahead [or rather, not given the don't-go-ahead] for Brian Yeomans to do his worst? And, by the same or a similarly incomprehensible process, Mark Richardson had also found out where Carol was living and was planning to visit her at any moment and hurt-or-worse her then grin at Eric?

He marvelled at his own irrationality but, unable to dispel it just by acknowledging its presence, decided to try and walk his worries off.

The morning was crisp under a bright azure sky. *The dogs will be cold,* he thought, the overriding thought in his general concern for them. He headed to the coastal village, taking the footpath through the trees rather than the road; it was too light, and he remained conscious of the importance of not being seen.

As he emerged through the swing gate at the end of the track, someone waved at him. It was the man he'd bought the scooter from. Eric made a feeble return gesture then quickly diverted down to the shore. The tide was coming in and the firth was filling up fast. The water at this point was like a two-headed snake, one head writhing towards the grassy tussocks bordering the land, the other twisting around the back of an elongated sandbank that ran parallel to the shoreline but about 20 metres out from it.

On the sandbank was a woman with a small girl. Eric watched them for a minute, wondering why the girl wasn't at school or nursery or somewhere, and if they knew about the incoming tide. The two heads of the snake would join up at any moment and the bank would become an inescapable island for the short time it would take the water to cover the top of the sand.

He was on the point of shouting at the pair when the woman, without warning, let go of the child's hand and began to run. She splashed through the rising current, leapt onto the bank, and kept running towards the footpath gate, slamming it behind her as she disappeared into the trees. The child, alone on the disappearing circle of solid ground, started to scream.

Eric looked around, hoping there was someone else at hand to stamp into the freezing water, preferably someone who knew what they were doing. There wasn't. The shore was deserted save for himself, the terrified child and, swooping above the galloping tide, the white gulls on breakfast reconnaissance.

Eric felt the perspiration slipping down his back go cold as it hit the icy air orbiting the gap between the bottom of his coat and the top of his trousers. He grasped at the trousers with one hand, using the other to jam coat, pullover, shirt, and vest into any slack in his waistband. Then he launched himself into the waves, snatched up the hysterical child and turned back to the shore. One foot sank into the mud, and he wrenched it out of his trapped shoe as the water reached the top of his knees.

Swinging the girl up onto his shoulders, he made a last desperate lunge for the bank, an awareness of the effects of the freezing water becoming apparent in the loss of feeling in his hands and lower limbs. He tumbled uncontrollably onto the white frosty grass and the girl slid from his neck and bounced on her head, landing in a silent, motionless heap beside him. Pushing back her matted hair, he saw the thin streak of blood across her blue-cold forehead and panicked that he might have failed; then her eyes opened, and she began to cry.

Eric gathered her to his quivering body as tightly as he could and slowly got to his feet. One shoe gone, he limped up the grassy bank, across the line of the footpath and out onto the road. He turned towards the village, clutching the girl, with some idea of knocking on all the front doors until he got a reply. However, before he reached the first house, a car overtook him and stopped. An attractive middle-aged woman got out of the driver's seat and walked back towards him.

"Are you alright?" she said. "Do you want to give me the little girl?"

Eric, teeth chattering and colder than he had ever been in his life, looked at her and hesitated. The woman fingered a laminated card on a lanyard round her neck.

"I'm with the local GPs' surgery," she said. "Doing my morning home visits. Why don't you both get in the car?"

As he handed the child over, his strength failed him, and he was overcome by dizziness. He fell to his knees, his hands flattening onto the bumpy road surface, and threw up. In amongst the familiar cream vegetably vomit, he thought he could make out streaks of black and red. Stringy viscose globules of snow fell from his nose like pouncing spiders, bouncing back up before they reached solid ground.

Eric felt the blanket being pulled over his heaving shoulders as he allowed himself to be guided into the doctor's car. In the back seat behind him, he heard the little girl whimpering fitfully but she at least sounded calmer. Beside him, in the driving seat, the doctor was on her phone. She paused to ask him a question.

"Where did you get the little girl?"

"In the water," he managed to reply through rigid-cold teeth. "A woman. Left. Her. Ran off."

"When was this?"

"Now. Just now. Girl was caught in tide coming in. Jumped in."

The doctor was speaking into her phone again, but he couldn't hear what she was saying through the thumping beat reverberating in his head.

She finished her call and switched on the car engine. Heat streamed through the dashboard vents and Eric felt a scintilla of feeling return to the ends of his fingers and begin to creep up his arms. He had a sense of being immersed in a sensory deprivation tank containing slowly warming water and, as the minutes ticked by, he gradually came back to life. When he raised his head, he saw that the doctor had the little girl in her arms and the child was sleeping peacefully.

"I'm Josephine," said the doctor. "That was a stupid thing to do, jumping in that water, but I'll forgive you seeing as how you saved this one's life."

Eric gave a short laugh and wiped his eyes before hearing another car pull up behind them. The doctor glanced over her shoulder and got out to greet the new arrival. Eric moved the driving mirror and saw her talking to a policeman. In the front seat of the police car, he saw the trembling figure of the woman who'd run away.

A moment later, the policeman walked round to Eric's door and opened it.

"Morning sir," he said in that officiously friendly tone adopted by TV detectives. "The doctor tells me you're the one who rescued the child. I'd like to get a few details from you,

[*no*, thought Eric, *let me out*]

but the doctor recommends we get you checked out at the hospital first.

[*we*, thought Eric, *we?* ***We?***]
She's going to drive you and the little girl in, and I'll be along shortly.

[*when you've talked to the attempted murderer sitting in your car,* thought Eric, *I trust you've locked her in there, oh there's more, he's not finished, go away, until I can escape*]

Is there anyone you need us to contact to say where you are?"
"No," said Eric. "Thank you."

[*He hadn't gone*]

"If I could just have your name, please, sir?"
"Rock," said Eric shakily. "Billy Rock."

**54**

This time, it just stopped. The pushing hands melted away and the corridor lit up again. Jane Shepherd took him by the arm and guided him back into her room.

"What happened?" said Terry.

"I suppose I could ask the same question," she said. "How are you feeling?"

"Fine," he said. "Better than. It's how it seems to work. When I come back from wherever I've been, I feel refreshed. Invigorated. At the risk of sounding like someone in a bad sci-fi book, how long was I out this time?"

"How long did it feel like?"

"Dunno. Ten, fifteen minutes."

"About 20 seconds," she said. "Where were you going just now before you came back…woke up?"

"Into the kitchen or up to the bedroom, I think," he said.

She gave him a quizzical look.

"Things from when I was a kid," he said. "Everything's to do with childhood, isn't it?"


[*The bedroom. More of that irritating present historic…*]

Terry, 18 months? Two? Young enough to still be in a cot, has been taken into his parents' bed for the night and is snuggled between them. Head against the outside wall of the bedroom, he sees his mother to his left, facing away from him. To his right, his father, lying on his back, snoring and, beyond him, the closed, curtained window looking down onto the narrow [still not tarmacked] cobbled street of tight terraced two-bedroom houses. Next-to-no cars then. Orange streetlights flickering ineffectively atop council-blue metal lamp standards. Cats galloping between the cuts leading to the back lanes. A locked-out dog, at the far end where the washed-down rail bridge used to be, howling hungrily.

Terry, awake, feels himself moving but the thick, coarse [pre-duvet] blankets remain still. He is floating above the bed, looking down on his parents and, between them, himself. Something is guiding him towards the window. Years later, he will see white blood vessels skitter across his eyeballs on bright days, maggot-like, and be reminded of this something. He is conscious of an attempt to manipulate him through the curtains because he can now see the street, wet with earlier evening rain.

All at once, he realises that he mustn't allow himself to be taken outside. He begins to fight the white abductors, resisting their coiling and re-grouping as he twists backwards, not going any further, not passing through the glass, glancing left and right and seeing unformed translucent faces, silent screaming in an agony which visibly increases the harder he tries to stay in the bedroom.

It is the first time he is aware of willpower, determination, mortality, vulnerability. To leave with the maggoty spirits is to die so don't leave, don't die. Not yet.

He asserts his strength, his mind and the faces fade and he slow-dives back down into himself and sleeps until morning. This wasn't a dream. It has never happened again [*yet*]but he thinks it will, must, at the final, unresistable end.


[*The kitchen*]


Terry, now nine? Ten? A bigger house, on a road now, promotion from a street. Three bedrooms and three children. His parents in one, baby sister in the smallest, him and younger brother in the back one with the view across the gardens.

His brother beside him in the bed, weak-chested and asthmatic, nightly struggling for breath, Terry awake and listening, ready to act [but not sure how/what] if the struggle should be lost.

Regularly, for two, three years, eventually falling asleep then wakened by raised voices from downstairs, is it his parents arguing? they're always arguing, his mother sometimes pulls her hair out and thrusts it at them all, *See what your father's made me do*, pronounced *Fah-Th, Th, Throw the hair on the fire, see it frizzle and sizzle, hiss into black oblivion*. The voices are stopping him from hearing fraternal breath-struggles so **they** must be silenced.

He throws his feet to the bedroom floor, teddies and gonks tumbling to the carpet, and creeps out and down the stairs. The door at the bottom is closed on a smoothly-balled catch. He pushes at it and is in the living-room.

His parents are smoking, watching TV, squeaking in patent leather armchairs, not seeing him. The voices are coming from behind the kitchen door. He crawls across the ripped-but-black-taped-up back of the settee, hoists himself up on the silver kitchen door handle, paint-edged, should have taken it off when decorating, never works to try and go round it.

Pushing the door, another smooth-ball catch, it opens into the parallel, night-time kitchen, not the neat table and four chairs day one with the cupboard with Dad's home-brew in it, this one with the cauldron and shelves of jars with doll-like but real baby limbs floating inside them.

[*How many limbs can a person lose before they stop being a person?* Terry will always ask himself forever after, for ever after.]

Every time, he tries his best not to make a sound because he wants to see what is in the cauldron, big, black, bubbling, no visible heat source. Every time, he fails.

One creak and they appear, sharp-faced, pointed hats, cackles, tight eyes finding him, moving towards him, pointed fingers stretching out, never touching because. He. Always. Wakes. Up. In the kitchen. The day kitchen at night. Back through the living-room. No TV, no parents but lingering smoke. They went to bed hours ago. They weren't there when he came down, but he saw them anyway.

Each time, he gets older and bolder and starts to double back, double-check that the kitchen is empty, is day kitchen. The last time, he is furtive. He sneaks back slowly, quietly, doesn't make a sound at last. Pushes the door open. They *are* there, waiting in the spaces between seconds, able to see us but we can't see them. Terry *has* seen them. They see him seeing, they point, hats, noses, spiny sharp fingers, converging on him. He grabs, touches one. They go. Like the maggoty spirits, the translucent agonised faces, he has faced and resisted them.

There will be more challenges to come.

# 55

Eric Bell and the little girl sat in Accident and Emergency and watched Josephine the GP as she spoke to the nurse on the reception counter. Coloured digital displays above the counter linked to the lights outside various anterooms and told you how long you could expect to wait to be seen. With the qualifier that unforeseen emergencies would push you back down the queue.

A long time ago, Eric had brought his daughter here with a burn from a dropped hot poker. Those were the days when putting the fire on took an hour's preparation rather than twisting a knob or pressing a button. He could still see the thin girl with the barely scraped face from a bicycle tumble, late teens, eight or nine years older than his daughter; could still hear her loud, whiny, attention-seeking voice,

"I've been here nearly an hour already. I need to be seen."

When she was eventually called, before going in to see the doctor, she began an unwelcomed public rant about what a terrible hospital this was. She was still speaking when the emergency doors at the back of the room pulled open and a body-laden trolley guided by two nurses and two ambulance crew (pre-paramedics?) usurped scraped-face as it rapidly entered the treatment area she'd just been assigned. Instead of sitting down again, she followed the trolley in, declaiming about her rights.

Seconds later, she emerged, pale and tearful, and ran out of the hospital. The local newspaper the next evening told of the woman, walking her daughter home from school, struck by a portable toilet that detached from the car towing it and mounted the pavement. The woman had been rushed to hospital but died shortly after arriving.

Eric [still] often wondered about the girl with the scraped face and the whiny voice, following the trolley into the room; had she learnt a lesson for life that day or reverted to the selfish complainer she'd been when she first came in?

Today, Josephine the GP had Eric and the child waved through for immediate examination by Dr Sumaiya Khatun, one of the white-coated duty staff. In here was another row of chairs outside a curtain-fronted cubicle. Eric sat on one whilst Sumaiya and a nurse took the girl into the cubicle and Josephine the GP departed to drive back to the coast and resume her home visits.

He felt the wetness stubbornly clinging to his legs below the knees, even though he had been provided with dry surgical hoses and slippers, all they had available in the hospital. His remaining shoe and saturated socks were stuffed into the pocket of his muddy coat.

The waiting area was in a space with three corridors and a staircase leading from it to other parts of the labyrinthine building. Eric Bell, growing agitated at the prospect of inevitable further questions, stood up and walked to the bottom of the stairs, intending to make his exit, when he heard the nurse call him.

"Mr Rock! The doctor would like to check you over now."

He was tempted to run for it, but his well-developed sense of caution led him into the cubicle as the nurse brought the little girl out. The child looked up at him, her face pale.

"'Bye 'bye," the girl said.

"I'm taking Dawn to her gran who's come for her, aren't I, Dawn?"

The curtain closed and Eric turned to the doctor.

"Is the kid OK?"

"She's fine," said Sumaiya. "A small bump on the head and a scratch. We'll keep an eye on her for now until we find out where she belongs."

"I think the police have the woman who abandoned her," said Eric.

Sumaiya sidestepped the remark.

"Let's have a look at you," she said.

She checked his blood pressure, shone a light in his eyes and listened to his heart.

"Can I go now?" he said as she continued to press the stethoscope to his chest.

"Mmm," she said. "Let me listen to that again."

It wasn't the best thing to say to someone in the circumstances and Eric felt his pulse quicken as his hand instinctively began to claw across his head.

"Is there something wrong?" he said.

"A little irregularity in the heartbeat."

"It's been a stressful morning," said Eric.

She was good at ignoring statements.

"I think we should send you for an ECG. I'll take some blood too if you don't mind."

The nurse came back in and whispered something to Sumaiya, who turned to Eric.

"The police are here and would appreciate a quick word with you."

"What about the ECG?" said Eric.

"I'll arrange that for when you come back. Alison will take you to them."

The nurse led him up one of the corridors and, in the distance, Eric saw the main Reception desk. Two uniformed police officers, neither of whom he'd seen before, were standing waiting. Eric went cold. The myth of Billy Rock would, he knew, be shattered in seconds.

"Thanks, er, Alison," he said to the nurse. "I see them. I'll be fine. You can leave me."

"Are you sure, Mr Rock?" she said.

"Of course," he said. "See you shortly."

She turned and left him. *It's like walking to your execution*, he thought, *but without the priest*.

He looked for possible ways out but there were none. Reaching the end of the corridor, one of the police officers turned to him and smiled.

"Mr Rock?" she said.

"Sorry," said Eric, glancing behind to where a thin, unsteady, middle-aged man was following. "That might be him."

Eric swerved towards the doors of the main entrance and passed a couple coming from one of the other passageways into the atrium. The woman was wearing an NHS lanyard with an ID card attached. The man wasn't but Eric noticed him because of the long-puzzled look that appeared on his face, a look which followed Eric through the revolving doors and out of the hospital.

# 56

"That was Eric Bell," said Terry, almost to himself.

"Pardon?" said Jane Shepherd.

"Nothing," said Terry. "You know me and my seeing things."

"Well, yes," she said. "Now, you've got the appointment card but, if anything untoward happens before we next meet, ring the 24-hour helpline number on the bottom and someone will find me."

"Yes. Thanks," said Terry. "I mean it."

"We'll get to the bottom of it. I promise."

[*Do you do colonoscopies as well?* he couldn't stop himself thinking]

"Yes. Thanks. 'Bye."

The unstoppable affection he felt for her, that he knew he would feel for anyone genuinely interested in helping him disassemble his mental tumults, was overtaken by thoughts of Eric Bell.

Outside the hospital doors, through the hazy fug from the dozen smokers standing there in the cold, Terry scanned the long drive leading down to the main road. Dead Eric, the thin hospital galoshes giving him a Chaplinesque gait, was penguinning away at a rapid lick.

Preparing to set off in pursuit, Terry was distracted by the appearance of the two police officers from through the spinning doors. They too surveyed the path, but Eric was now concealed by an ambulance and the double-decker bus coming up the road. By the time the vehicles had gone, so had Eric.

"Is it worth getting the car, sarge?" Terry heard the male officer say.

"No. We're flying blind here. We don't even know what he looks like. It'd be more productive to go through the CCTV with the doctor."

They went back inside.

*At least*, thought Terry, *he wasn't a figment of my imagination. Eric Bell isn't dead.*

146

The now-confirmed-as-resurrected Eric, once clear of the hospital, considered his next move. He was 13 miles from home, penniless because he'd only intended going for a walk; phoneless because walking was for finding headspace; and wet and cold with the ridiculous hospital galoshes exposing him to every bump underfoot. He was also probably being sought by the police for what he considered to be mixed reasons: on one hand, a hero; on the other, an interview absconder. It was a bizarre situation.

He looked at the deepening December sky, newly plump with threatening snow. A mini-mart clock, sighted through gaudily decorated windows, told him there were less than three hours of what passed for daylight left. The obvious solution was to find Ernie, so he began a circumlocutory meander in the direction of the shop, avoiding main thoroughfares, people and possible police cars.

He walked past a backstreet newsagent, its metal-meshed local paper billboard screaming,

## HIT-AND-RUN DEATH
## DRIVER SOUGHT

*A tragedy for someone just before Christmas*, he thought before his mind flitted irrationally to the memory of his all-time favourite headline,

## CHICKEN FARMER ON FURTHER SEX CHARGES

and he reflected on what an odd machine the human being, is to be able to switch emotional responses so quickly and (maybe) callously.

Eric caught the lingering smell from a fish-and-chip shop, closed after lunchtime trading, and was seized with hunger. As the landscape darkened, he felt more and more in a dreamworld, even further detached from the already strange reality that was now his everyday life.

He had experienced peculiar days before, of course, but this was the oddest of all. A murder attempt thwarted; a life saved; a brief but unsettling medical examination; and here he was, a fugitive, *on the lam*, as the noir detectives would say. David Janssen's *Fugitive*, not Harrison Ford's. Eric had been a big fan of Janssen's show and remembered the actor's shockingly early death. From a heart attack, he was sure. What had Sumaiya the hospital doctor said?

"A little irregularity in the heartbeat."

and,

"I think we should send you for an ECG."

She was arranging it. Perhaps someone was still waiting beside a machine even now, unaware that Eric 'William Rock' Bell wasn't coming to be hooked up, assessed, diagnosed with *what?*

*Stop thinking about it*, thought Eric.

Impossible.

At last, he came to the back of Ernie's shop and tried the doorknob. It turned but the door was bolted. The yellow light glared out through the frosted panel at Eric's probing face. He tapped on the glass, the panic beginning to rise. He tried again, the taps rising into knocks that reverberated around the brick walls of the back yard. Ready to give up, his mouth dry, his forehead beginning to sweat, he felt all his readings abruptly stabilise as an indistinct shape loomed into view and the bolt was pulled back.

"Eric!" said Camilla, undoing the safety chain on the door. "Come in. Sit down. I won't be a minute."

It was as if he'd never been away, she was so natural in her manner.

When Eric first disappeared, Ernie had falsely promised he wouldn't make Camilla aware of the true situation. It didn't take long for the truth to emerge.

"Yes, I lied because you already had enough going on," said Ernie on an early caravan park visit, "but there was never any doubt in my mind that, if I was going to be your only link with your past life Eric, I needed to put Camilla in the picture. I wouldn't sneak around on her for anyone, not even you. She's as inscrutable as the Sphinx so you'll be completely safe. Besides, there might be emergency situations where she could help."

The revelation perversely reassured rather than upset Eric at the time, reinforced now by the realisation that here was such a situation.

Camilla vanished into the front of the shop, and he heard her closing up.

"It's only 3.45," he said as she came back through.

"I doubt if there'll be a big rush of customers on an afternoon like this."

She looked Eric over then went off again, this time up the tight little stairs leading to the storeroom above. When she came back down, she had a towel, clean jogging bottoms and a pair of trainers, which she threw into the small side-room replete with sink, shower, and toilet.

"While you sort yourself out," she said. "I'll make you a sandwich."

Warmed and cleaned, Eric sat at the kitchen table opposite Camilla and ate hungrily. Between mouthfuls of cheese and pickle, he recounted the events of the day so far.

"Things happen to you Eric," she said. "They always have."

He was halfway through his second mug of tea when they heard the shop door open and close, and Ernie came through.

"Hello Cam," he said, kissing her on the forehead. "And hello Eric. I thought it might be you."

Eric looked puzzled and Ernie unwrapped the rolled-up newspaper he was carrying.

"Late Final," he said. "Usually full of rubbish but today, two reasons to read it. Reason number one!"

He held the front page up. The photograph was low resolution, out of focus and taken from too high an angle for the face to be clear but, to anyone who knew him, it was quite possibly Eric Bell.

# 57

Terry never read the local paper. If he had, he too might have recognised the grainy image from the hospital CCTV camera under the bold type:

**MYSTERY HERO SAVES DROWNING CHILD**

He had returned home from the hospital and cooked the evening meal that he and Pat were now eating.

"Here's one for you," she said.

Terry smiled. It was her standard opening line to a story from work. Pat was a partner in a local firm of solicitors, an endless source of entertaining tales that Terry never failed to enjoy.

"A client wants to sue his lover because his lover – a man – has been unfaithful to him with a third man and may have contracted an STD that he may or may not have passed on to the client."

"There's a lot of 'mays' in there," said Terry.

"Stay with it," said Pat. "The thing is, the client and his lover are both married to women, but the client maintains that, as both marriages are allegedly sexless with the wives, they're irrelevant to the central breach of promise action the client wants to bring because his lover has broken their agreement to be monogamous and faithful to each other within their homosexual relationship. Got it?"

"I think so. Why did the lover have the fling?"

"Because he thought the client fancied someone else."

"Another man?"

"Of course."

"Did he?"

"Yes, and he apparently told his lover, but the client maintains that there was still no justification for the fling."

"Was it a big fling?"

"Two fumbles. In one night. A day or two after the client told the lover about fancying the other man."

"So, it was a revenge fling thing," said Terry.

"Yes," said Pat. "But there's one more circumstance to consider."

"I'm enthralled," said Terry. "Tell me."

"The client and lover have previously had a mutually consensual threesome with yet another man. However, that apparently doesn't contravene the fidelity agreement because they were both present and willing."

Pat slapped the table enthusiastically and Terry started to laugh.

"Are you going to take the case?" he said.

"Gilly's keen to give it a go," said Pat. "The folly of youth and all that. The defence will crucify her."

"It reminds me of all those debt cases at Citizens Advice," said Terry. "The ones where they wanted inconvenient debts written off but continue to borrow money for exciting new things. I think the legal term is 'having your cake and eating it'."

"There's plenty of cake around in this one, that's for sure," said Pat as the phone began to ring. She went into the hall to answer it.

"It's your friend, Mrs Green," she said when she came back in. "She's very excited about something. She's coming round to see you in about an hour."

Teresa Green arrived exactly as the hall clock struck seven. Pat showed her into the front room where Terry was ineptly stoking the fire in the grate. They'd only recently had the blocked chimney opened again and he hadn't yet quite got the hang of drawing the flames.

"I'll be upstairs working when you decide to make some coffee for us all Terry," said Pat.

"Do you mind?" said Teresa, taking the poker from Terry's hesitant hand. Wielding it like a magic wand, she coaxed the coal into yellow licking life.

"Where did you learn to do that?" said Terry.

"Oh, we women learned a lot of practical skills in the war," she said. "You had to to survive with all the men gone away."

Terry nodded sympathetically for a second then realised.

"The war? What war?"

She looked at him, eyes twinkling.

"Old people, eh? They can't do nuffink!"

She'd brought along the first edition of that day's evening paper and handed it to Terry. It was folded over so he could see the main story on Page 3. He read the report and looked at the two pictures, the one of the dual carriageways outside the castle and the other, the unsympathetic, aggressive headshot of the victim.

# 58

"Are they allowed to print a photo of me just like that?" said Eric. "Isn't there a data protection law? And it's from a camera in a hospital."

"They'd probably say it's in the public interest," said Ernie. "In any case, it's too late. They've done it."

Eric stared at the newspaper, hand sliding through hair again.

"Would you know it was me if you didn't know it was me?" said Eric.

"I don't really think so," said Camilla. "It's very grainy."

"And you're dead," said Ernie. "That could help."

"But nobody knows he's dead because nobody knows it's Eric," said Camilla, optimistically.

The report gave a very sketchy recap of the morning's events but no details of who the little girl or the woman who abandoned her were. It was slanted as a 'help us find this modest hero' story, and readers were urged to contact either the paper or the police if they recognised him as he could have 'further useful information regarding the investigation'. There was nothing about Eric doing a runner from the hospital.

"Gotta give 'em credit, it's audacious," said Ernie. "Bashed together, published and on-sale in, what, two or three hours?"

"But why?" said Eric.

"It has all those elements the readers love," said Camilla. "A child in danger saved by a mysterious stranger who then disappears. A homicidal mother, if it is the mother. Big back story to explore there. It sells last editions today, will be in again tomorrow with a few more details and, by way of a bonus, gets the readers to do the police's work for them and find you. There's nothing unusual about any of this. It'll push sales up for weeks if they string it out properly."

Eric stared at her.

"Cam once worked for the *Daily Mail*," said Ernie. "She knows the game."

"In fact," said Camilla, "without wanting to worry you Eric, it's exactly the kind of story the nationals are likely to pick up on."

Eric, almost impossibly, went an even paler shade of white and began pushing *both* hands through his hair.

"I can't even go back to the caravan," he said. "The police'll be looking for me all over the area."

"Did you tell anybody you lived round there?" said Camilla. "The doctor or the police?"

"No," said Eric. "By the time I met them, I was too cold to talk."

He looked hopeful for a moment.

"Do you think I'd be OK to go back?"

"It's a difficult one," said Camilla, "but I'd say yes. Just keep your head down for a week or two."

"While we're thinking about it," said Ernie, "let me present you with the *other* noteworthy story in this hideous rag."

Ernie picked the newspaper up from the table and folded the front page over before setting it down again. The headline Eric had seen on the display board earlier stared out at him from Page 3.

## HIT-AND-RUN DEATH
## DRIVER SOUGHT

Eric was too consumed with his current predicament to take any real interest until Ernie pointed to the photograph of the victim, then he began to read avidly.

*A man killed after a suspected hit-and-run accident on Castle Way at about 1pm yesterday has been identified as 39-year-old Mark Richardson, believed to be from the Currock area of the city.*

*Witnesses claim that Mr Richardson stumbled into the road near traffic lights on a controversial new pedestrian crossing and was struck by a car which failed to stop. He was taken to hospital with life-threatening injuries but died soon afterwards.*

*A black Ford Focus was later found abandoned behind the castle. A witness claimed that Mr Richardson had been drinking and was involved in a fracas with another man shortly before the incident.*

*Detective Sergeant Roger Wallbridge, of the police's Collision Investigation Unit, said,*

*'We are still trying to establish exact details of this tragic occurrence and would urge anyone with further information to contact us.'*

He re-read the story several times then looked up at Camilla and Ernie, an expression of complete bewilderment on his face.

"After all that, he gets killed in a fluke road accident. It's too much to take in."

The day had taken its toll on Eric, and he was in no condition to go back to the caravan site and spend the night alone so, despite their mutual decision never to do it, Eric accepted Ernie's offer to stay at the house.

Later, with Eric upstairs in the guest bedroom, Ernie and Camilla considered the situation.

"It's all changed Cam," said Ernie. "Just like that."

"It had to at some point," she said. "Something was bound to happen eventually. What does he do next? Find Carol?"

"It's complicated, isn't it?" said Ernie. "But at least Richardson's out of the picture. That's one big problem gone."

"The family won't rest till they find the driver," said Camilla.

"That car won't have a current registration, the chassis number will have been filed off and Shane Yeomans'll be in Portugal by now," said Ernie. "I doubt if they'll be looking for him there. And, in the highly unlikely event anybody does make a link, there's no law against those witnesses being friends of Brian."

Eric, meanwhile, lay back on the bed and tried to relax but couldn't. He was feeling a little nudged-along-the-shelf today, with a deepened sense of losing what little control he had over his life and the events in it. The worrying about what might happen never left him, had been with him since childhood. It wasn't by choice, but he knew he was – as Camilla had said – one of those people that things happen to, and not usually in a good way. Mark Richardson had gone, though Eric doubted it was an accident that had carried him off. And tomorrow, there'd be more on his act of heroism in the paper.

*As one problem's solved, another develops*, he thought, too exhausted to sleep. *When will it ever end?*

# 59

The following day, Terry went for a swim at the local pool. It was something he did when he had a rare full hour free at lunchtime. The pool was new but housed in a sandstone Victorian building with,

## MUNICIPAL BATHS & WASH HOUSES

carved above the entrance. He liked the way old and new collided in the design. It was like life, like time. Time.

There was no point arriving before noon because the pool was blocked off for an hour at the end of each weekday morning for a specific group of swimmers. Today, it was PENSIONERS HOUR and Terry always speculated on the spelling of the sign. Did PENSIONERS need an apostrophe and, if it did, where?

*How many pensioners?* he wondered.

He was enough of a regular to have struck up a casual changing-room acquaintance with some of the PENSIONERS, one or two of whom told him they'd like to be rebranded as SENIORS.

"SENIORS would make you sound like you're in charge whereas PENSIONERS gives the impression of a bunch of doddery old gits," Bob had said the first time he'd encountered Terry.

Bob was here today.

"How do boy," he said. "Water's a bit cold for my liking this fine morn."

"Geordie not here today?"

"No. He's been called into the infirmary for tests."

"What kind of tests?"

"It doesn't matter," said Bob. "When you get to our age, if a doctor calls you in for tests, you're probably fucked."

"Any progress on the knees?" said Terry.

Bob was 83 and his knees were bad enough to give him gip but not bad enough for the hospital to replace them, so he was going private.

"Now if I was some fat young bird whose legs were collapsing because I couldn't stop filling my face with cream cakes, I could probably get 'em done tout suite and for free. But the NHS doesn't want to waste cash on old farts like me," he'd told Terry and Terry found Bob's disregard for appropriate terminology both refreshing and amusing.

This morning, though, Bob did look very uncomfortable.

"The right one's started giving way without notice. If I wasn't so careful about staying close to things I can grab, I'd have had a nasty accident by now. Though that might have persuaded them to do something. As it is, I've got the private place lined up for early February."

"Are they doing them both?"

"No. It's about thirteen grand apiece. I'll get the worst one done and save up for the other out of the pension."

"How long's that going to take?"

"Two, three years. Though I could save the expense completely."

"How?" said Terry.

"By dying," said Bob with a dry laugh.

As Terry jumped into the deep end, thoughts began swirling like the water around his arms. Teresa Green had come round the night before to show him the article on the hit-and-run.

"This Mark Richardson was the brother of the late Lewis Richardson," she said. "The one who killed Alice Cooper. Who was convicted partly because of your friend Eric Bell?"

Terry found this very interesting.

"Do you have some theory about the accident?" he said.

"More an intuition," she said. "I was on the force a long time and you get a smell for things. Lewis Richardson kills Alice and is put inside. He gets out and soon afterwards Eric Bell moves away. Lewis dies of the brain thing and Eric moves back. Now, as I said before, Mark maybe takes over the getting back at Eric and that leads Eric to disappear, probably to protect his wife. Latest thing is Mark's dead."

Terry had looked at her in anticipation.

"It wouldn't surprise me," she said, "if Eric Bell was to reappear."

"If he did, wouldn't another Richardson go after him?"

"I doubt it," she said. "Mark was one on his own. Obsessive. Psychotic. Clever?"

"Clever?"

"Instinctively. We had him down for all sorts of things, but he always managed to avoid getting caught. The younger Richardsons have got enough troubles of their own without taking on mad Uncle Mark's as well."

"But Eric Bell doesn't know that."

"No, but he might risk it after a month or two."

Terry was thinking about this as he swam relentlessly up and down the pool. What he wasn't thinking about was the fuzzy picture of Eric Bell on the front of last night's paper because he hadn't seen it. Teresa Green had bought the earlier edition.

After 50 lengths, he got out. He wasn't needed at work until 2.00 and it was barely past 12.30 so he went to visit his mother.

She was sitting in her chair in the living-room, the fire and television turned up full, and barely acknowledged him. It was one of her ways of dealing with the loneliness of her life since Terry's dad had died: keep any emotions as contained as you can. He sat on the settee and waited in what was a familiar routine. Eventually, she said.

"Well, are we having a cup of tea or not?"

"We are," said Terry, getting up to make it. There was a click from the front porch.

"That'll be tonight's paper," she said. "Fetch us it through first. It's late today. He must have a boy off."

"It's an evening paper but late because it arrives at dinnertime," said Terry, who shared her view that dinnertime was in the middle of the day and teatime was when people who thought themselves better than they were ate dinner.

*We'll deal with supper separately*, flashed through his head

"It usually comes first thing in the morning," she said. "That's what I'm saying. Jimmy must have a boy off."

Jimmy, the newsagent, was one of a long rollcall of his mother's community contacts that Terry had never or only briefly met but who populated the vast majority of conversations he had with her. Like many people Terry came across, his mother talked about herself and rarely asked him about his life but, unlike most of the others, Terry didn't mind. He liked to hear about the comings and goings, the minutiae of her existence because it meant she had something to think about. Not enough but something.

He came back in, handed her the paper, and went into the back kitchen to put the kettle on. As he was dropping the teabags into the mugs – he always had the *World's Greatest Dad* one he'd bought all those years ago for the World's Greatest Dad – his mother shouted through to him.

"Terry! Come here a minute."

"The tea's nearly done."

"Aye, leave it a second. Come and see this."

She was holding up the paper. The grainy photo from yesterday's Late Final cover was on today's first edition.

"What you were saying the other day about Eric Bell. If I didn't know he was dead, I'd swear this was him."

# 60

As Terry was swimming, Ernie was yet again driving Eric out to the caravan site. When they reached the entrance road, Ernie pulled into the waterlogged lay-by used by dog walkers and switched off the engine.

The police forensics team that Eric was half-expecting was nowhere to be seen. The road and the park were as deserted as they had been since the clocks went back. The mile between here and the scene of Eric's heroic act was evidently far enough to inhibit official investigations, at least for now.

The pair walked down to Eric's caravan and went inside. The plan had been to scope the place out, see how safe it looked, then decide whether to relocate Eric. So far, it looked as if no immediate action was required.

"You can stay with us as long as you like, you know," said Ernie.

"I do know, and I appreciate it," said Eric. "But you've already done too much these past months. I wouldn't feel happy imposing on you anymore."

"When would you feel happy Eric?" said Ernie gently.

Eric looked away into the unseeable distance leading to his future.

After Ernie left, Eric packed his small rucksack and locked up the caravan. His resolve couldn't be described as firm but his need to act, to move things on, was unwavering. He had promised to spend Christmas with Ernie and Camilla to assuage their evident worries about him. That gave him five days in which to do something definite.

He waited until the light was going then pulled open the storage box holding the scooter. Locking up both box and caravan, he started up the bike and set off. Swirls of snow were whisking above the firth but other than that the landscape seemed fixed, bleak, and motionless, paralysed by the icy touch of winter's fingers.

In town, he squeezed in between the barrier and the gatepost of the biscuit factory car-park and locked the machine in the shed at the back. He'd spotted the yard on his amblings the day before and it seemed an ideal place to hide the scooter: private yet busy, and big enough for no one to take notice of an anonymous old bike like his.

Pressing the seat back down over the stored helmet, he headed for the railway station. Its brightly lit entrance hall contained a newsagent on one side and ticket offices on the other and he was mortified to see the rack of evening papers. His hazy image was splashed over the front page, seemingly lying in wait for him.

Forsaking the manned counters for the automatic machines, he pulled his hat down low and pushed his scarf over his mouth as he selected his ticket. Pressing 'Confirm', his heart started as the 'Cards only' sign flashed up on the display. He had no card, only the diminishing reserves of banknotes in his pocket and the old leather bag tucked into the roof panel of the caravan. It was yet another confirmation of his invisibility in a me-centred world.

A voice from behind startled him.

"Do you need assistance, sir?"

The red-coated customer care girl ['Operative'? 'Helper'? 'Support staff'? What did you call anyone these days?] was at his shoulder. He mumbled something incoherent and pointed at the message.

"Ah, that sometimes happens," she said. "Sorry about that but you can use the manned booths instead."

She swept away to deal with another minor crisis, leaving Eric flummoxed and staring at the screen. He touched the 'Start Again' option and re-entered the information. The 'Cards Only' light had gone out and he watched with relief as the slot swallowed his paper money. He took his tickets and looked at the Departures board. Trains were delayed due to a power failure further up the line.

Keeping his head angled, he headed to the toilet on the platform and locked himself in a cubicle as hailstones began to ricochet off the glass roof above. He took stock of himself: sitting on a toilet, trousers up, in a cold railway station on a dark December afternoon, his picture peeping out from the evening paper, waiting for a train that might never arrive.

*You're living the dream, Eric*, he thought ruefully. *Living the dream.*

Terry said to his mother,

"If *you* know it's Eric Bell, surely others will as well."

"It's a long time since he lived round here," she said. "There's hardly anybody left from then. And most people who knew him will be thinking he died in the floods. That's what I thought till you brought him up. Somebody from where he moved to might recognise him, but I doubt it. When you're gone, you're gone these days. Anyway, it might not be him."

Terry did a couple of small jobs for her then set out to walk back to work. He couldn't stop himself from going over what his mother had said: *When you're gone, you're gone these days.*

It seemed at odds with a world full of people continually trying to immortalise themselves but, when you examined her comment more closely, it made sense: the more instantaneous everything became, the less enduring. Your photo on today's screens was gone by tomorrow, replaced by someone very like you. In the past [*my God, I am getting old*, thought Terry, *IN THE PAST?*], you knew your neighbours, neighbourhood, friends, scrotes, the whole community. They had a solidity, a permanence, they existed, and you could *touch* them. [*Better not try that these days*].

*And yet*, thought Terry, *and yet...* and he [not **me**, my head, it has a mind of its own] was off again, rolling around in a big key-lidded tin of cod philosophy.

He'd had that idea once, to adapt online selling to value famous people at different stages in their trajectory of public visibility and acclaim:

**ELVIS '56** [*New, hot, exciting, bigger than anything*] Prime condition, $60,000,000

*Or*

**ELVIS '75** [*Bored, running to seed, a dancing chicken but reliable earning potential*] Acceptable condition, $100,000 o.n.o.

*Or*

**ELVIS '78** [*Dead, bigger than ever, guaranteed long-term, no-risk investment*] Serious offers only.

Who, anywhere, held their value?

Walking towards the office now, into the town, he was seeing ghosts. That was Barry and Freda Weston he'd just passed. Once upon a time, they'd lived over the road with their two sons, both around Terry's age but never really his friends because Barry and Freda didn't let them out of the garden to play. Like dogs, except they used the indoor toilet.

One of the boys – Craig – was terrified of going to sleep from the first day he realised he might not wake up *[Had transparent wormy spirits tried to get Craig out of the bedroom window too? Where is he so I can ask him?]*

Barry would sometimes come over and help Terry and his dad fix cars on the path. He was very strong then but one day, aged 35, his heart stopped for no reason* and he was rushed away in an ambulance. Next time he appeared, he was diminished, thinner, weak, his hair gone from brown to white, like autumn to winter. Nobody thought he would last and yet here he was today, his whiteness now shrouding his whole being and body, still with Freda [also, but not quite as, white], when many tougher specimens had shuffled off years ago.

*[Alan Johnston's dad, Buddy Holly specs, best-looking wife around, hosepipe on full, the foaming water washing away the blood from the head wound sustained from collapsing on the path. For no reason. *]*

Terry, walking and thinking wildly. Thinking about dying will drive you mad. Not thinking about it means you're mad already. We're all a multiplying version of former selves and where are the joins, where's the move from one to another? When was the exact moment you ceased to be young, fast, middle-aged, handsome [if you ever were], attractive, VISIBLE? If you saw the transitions as they happened, it was acceptable. Compare and contrast, though, with that thought-lost individual who reappears after 10, 20 years, the same but not the same.

Falling-off-the-edge-of-living-memory actor, Spencer Tracy, filming a transformation scene in *Dr Jekyll & Mr Hyde* (1941) was visited by the film's producer, not a fan:

"Which one's he being now?"

A good question for us all.

Terry, needing to hurry, took a short cut past the biscuit factory. And there he is. Ain't that him? Ain't that Eric Bell, galumphing out of the carpark? The two of them, almost simultaneously looking at their watches [*who has a watch anymore?*], Eric thinking of timetables and connections, Terry wondering if being late back to work is worth the trouble of knowing where Eric is going next.

# 62

An almost-empty service arrived, and Eric Bell got on through the bottom door of the rear carriage. It was only when he had sunk into a window seat in the very last row that he felt able to again expose his head to the outside world. He watched the snow blow up into a blizzard, hiding the fell tops as the train rattled down the West Coast main line, gradually losing time. An hour later, they slowed onto the bridge over the river and glided into the station where he had to run to catch his connection.

Drawing up once again at the seaside platform, he still wasn't entirely sure what he was going to do next. In truth, he hadn't thought beyond lurching back in Carol's direction in the hope that inspiration for some kind of strategy would descend when (or preferably before) he reached her. Now he was here, and it hadn't.

Desultorily, he headed for the promenade as the last gasp of light between the bobbling clouds and the black outline of the horizon was extinguished. The supermarket, now unashamedly festive, shone out like the one beacon of hope in the ravaged town. Nearing the entrance, he stopped, started, stopped, ravished his hair, started… repeating then, in despair, crossing over the road.

He pressed his stomach against the rusting rails overlooking the beach, letting the cold metal sink into his covered flesh in an effort to rouse himself to action. Once again, he was faced with a choice and didn't know what to do. He rocked back and forwards, frustrated and hating himself.

"They're not safe," came the voice. "Metal fatigue. Bounce too hard and you'll be into that water. For real, this time."

He turned, held up his quivering arms, head shaking, unable to stop the flow from his too-heavy eyes. A roar of pain came from him and pitched across the stormy tide. Then he fell onto her shoulder.

"You're alright Eric," said Carol. "Let's go home."

He sat on the settee, waiting for her to come back in. They'd walked arm in arm, silently, along the prom, the questions in his head refusing to take voice.

She laid the tray on the table, the cups clattering together. He watched as she poured the tea, seemingly unconcerned, and this simple act unleashed all the shame and doubt he'd been holding inside since the day he decided to die.

"Carol…" he began but she pressed a finger to his lips.

"Drink, Eric. You're freezing. Get warm first."

She was wearing her work overall and went out to get changed. When she came back, she sat beside him and took his hand. He raised his head like a schoolboy in disgrace.

"How long have you known?" he said.

"I never thought you'd died," she said. "At first, I was in denial. Full of a sort of desperate hope. You hear of people who go missing and the relatives *want* a body to be found. It gives them closure, as they say these days. Well, I *didn't* want you to be found because that meant you were still alive. Then there was that day at the train when I thought I saw you."

"You did," said Eric. "When I saw you, I could hardly stand it."

"That's why I sent the note to the house. 'Hello Eric?' I was hoping to smoke you out."

"In a roundabout way, it worked. I knew I had to see you, but I couldn't because…"

Words failed him and he gazed at her helplessly.

"I've never doubted you're a good man Eric," she said. "I know there's a reason why you did what you did. It'll come out when you're ready."

"I can't expect you to just take me back on Carol," he said. "Not after how I must have hurt you."

"As my mother always said, let me be the judge of that."

She didn't press him, details of her life since Eric's disappearance serving to fill the empty silences borne of his embarrassment and regret. It was close to what he'd deduced: her not wanting to stay in their home but still wanting to be in a place where they had a shared history. The house they were in now belonged to someone Carol had worked with when they were here before but currently living abroad. In return for looking after the place and the other tenants, she paid a very low rent. Eric's life insurance had paid off what little was left of the mortgage on their family property, and there had been a substantial lump sum when the court finally confirmed his death. Carol hadn't touched this, hadn't sought the confirmation but had accepted it as the sensible way forward.

Eventually, Eric felt ready to try and explain. It came as no surprise to her that his actions proceeded from the Lewis Richardson trial. She'd seen how he'd been affected, was willing to move away, then back... There were no recriminations or criticism of his decisions, not even of his inability to discuss his thoughts and feelings with her.

"You've never been a talker," she said. "I've always known that too."

As Eric told her about the latest developments – the hit-and-run, the drowning child, the front-page photo – they at last reached the crucial question: what to do now?

# 63

Terry Ellis followed Eric as far as the railway station before asking himself why. Idle curiosity? Like Teresa Green, he had no intention of taking anything further. Based on the little he knew about Eric Bell, bolstered with a pinch of deduction and conjecture, he could understand why the man might have decided to disappear. Others might be tempted to confront or expose him, but such a notion was abhorrent to Terry, who viewed life as difficult enough already without nosey outsiders interfering.

He went back to work but knew it was one of those days when you can't settle. Having missed the start of the 2pm meeting he was '*expected to attend*' [he knew it was wrong: dereliction of duty, unprofessional, all that, but he wasn't good with *expectations* like this], he decided he might as well break in a few minutes late as sit at his desk staring blankly at things to do that wouldn't be done today.

It was being held in the large conference room and this meant he couldn't avoid being seen as the only entrance was to the side of the lectern where the speaker stood. From the notice on the outside of the double doors, Terry was reminded that the meeting was about potential redundancies. He knew this was an issue of great significance to the majority of his colleagues, but he found it, like so much of life at present, hard to care about.

*Would like to get out of this place though*, he thought.

As he went in, the Senior Manager looked up from his notes and scowled. Terry was cheered by this sign of obvious disapproval and took the end seat in the noticeably underpopulated front row. The old boy resumed but Terry was unable to zone in what he was talking about. The voice was like a bagpipe drone, a tuneless accompaniment to a lousy song.

Terry looked around at his colleagues, practised expressions of interest failing to conceal obvious discomfiture at their potential removal from not only their jobs but also this really rather pleasant [*and, today, nice in the winter, saves the heating at home, warm*] building. In his head, he conducted a little straw poll on his fellow workers: how many did he like? [*not many, no you have to give a proper answer, **two**], actively dislike? [**two**, there's balance for yah*]; what about the others? [*they're here, they're OK, they sort of know what they're doing, it's all Emperor's New Clothes*]; who would you get rid of? [*myself first, and then old Emperor Penguin himself, the boring, fucking useless twat now addressing us*].

### *Must try and concentrate. What IS he banging on about?*

"…and to give you fuller details of the redundancy process, I'll hand you over to my colleague, Priscilla from HR."

*Missed the starter*, thought Terry, *but the main course is the important one.*

Priscilla was no easier to listen to than Penguin, but she at least looked better [*not allowed, Terry, now against the law to think that, objectifying her because of her tight but voluminous arse*]. She outlined and underlined and clarified processes and procedures and phases, none of it making any sense but at least not sounding like bagpipes.

*More like an oboe, haut-bois en Frenchie, high wood, High Wood If I Could*, thought Terry, *but [butt] I Can't Sew I Won't.*

Terry's attention switched back to the Penguin. His introductory duties accomplished [and *his* job safe, they always are, that lot make up the rules to suit themselves, suit yourself in a Penguin Suit], he was now sitting on a plush padded chair behind Priscilla, fiddling with his phone.

When she'd finished her spiel, Priscilla asked if there were any questions.

"When will the redundancy process begin?" [from Howard Whatmough, *Wattabore* in Terry's head, his office next-door neighbour, *she's just told you, immediately, you could go now, and nobody would notice never mind miss you, good gawd*]

"How will payment packages be calculated?" [from that woman two offices down, Amy, the one with the union rep husband who always makes sure he's away on business during industrial action, so *he* never loses his day's wages and, again, Priscilla's already explained it all but Amy's ignorance is forgivable because she's got *something life-limiting*. **Death**, that's life-limiting]

"Why is Our Leader fiddling with his phone even as his staff's very destinies are being discussed?"

*Who asked that very good question?* thought Terry, looking round again.

Everyone was trying not to stare at him. The Phone Fiddler, taken unawares, appeared confused.

"Any more questions?" said Priscilla hopefully.

"Will there…?" began a voice from the back [that idiot who got to be a professor despite being semi-literate and proud of it].

"Hang on," said the voicer of the Very Good Question. "We haven't had the answer to the phone fiddling query yet."

There was much embarrassed coughing, gaze-averting, it's not happening, please shut up. Terry looked at the Penguin who'd slid his phone into his pocket and now stood up.

"I think this may be a good moment to terminate the meeting," he said.

"Coming from you, 'I think' is an oxymoron," said the questioner. "Where's your respect for your professional colleagues?"

Silence.

"What's my name?" persisted the troublesome inquisitor.

"Pardon?"

"We've worked together for several years. Who am I?"

Silence.

"And that," said the niggler, pointing at the Senior Manager, "is why we're in the old poo-poo. You don't know who half of us are, don't care about us and only got the management job because it meant you didn't inflict reputational damage on this place through your inability to deal effectively with our client base."

"Terry."

Terry looked at the woman sidling up to him. Kate. One of the two people here he actively liked.

"Just a second," he said to her then, turning back to the Penguin. "So, if the redundancies are to be competence-based, you're the one to go. Or are you on commission related to how much money you can save this laughable institution?"

"Terry," Kate said again and again before the darkness descended and he was gone into it.

Later, but not sure how much. His name again but a different voice.

"Terry?"

Pat was looking down on him, his liked colleague standing behind her. He was in the staff room feeling comfortable.

"Kate rang me at work. She said you were behaving strangely in a meeting."

"Was I?" said Terry to Kate. "It all made sense to me. What was strange was that no one else joined in."

"People are scared," said Kate. "They've got commitments, families, responsibilities. They don't want the applecart upturned. Especially not by the truth."

She smiled but she was patronising him and he realised his liking and respect for her was now diminished.

"So how did I get back here?" he said.

"On your own. I just suggested you might want to take a moment and you left. I followed you."

"Was I angry?"

"No, perfectly calm," she said. "And that made it a little bit scarier."

Pat drove him home. It was becoming something of a habit. She said nothing until they were in the house, then,

"We've got to get to the bottom of this. You need to ring that direct number Mrs Dalzell gave you."

"First thing in the morning," he said. "I promise. Though I didn't say anything unreasonable or untrue in that meeting."

"No," said Pat. "Kate didn't say you had. But it's as if your brakes are failing. Let's get them fixed before the car goes over the cliff."

<h1 style="text-align:center">64</h1>

It was Friday morning, the last before Christmas, and the white-headed waves vomited over the seawall onto the red granite path. Bobbing boats, toy-like, pogoed in the grey water, tethered to the shifting whispering sands beneath by deep curvaceous anchors. Eric Bell, bent against the spitting gale, dropped onto the wooden bench on the calmest side of the Clock Tower and found his phone.

"Hello," he said. "Ernie, I've met Carol. She knows the lot. I'm down here with her now. No, she's not actually beside me. She's had to go to work. I'm on the prom. Skegness is so bracing and all that."

When the call ended, Ernie went upstairs to the bathroom to find Camilla.

"Eric's met up with Carol. He's told her the whole story."

"The *whole* story?" she said.

"Well, as much as *he* knows."

"How did she take it?"

"He didn't say but he didn't have to. I haven't heard him sound so happy in years. No, forget the 'so'. I don't believe he's been happy at all since Alice Cooper died."

"What next?" said Camilla.

"Cam," said Ernie, "you just have a special genius for nailing the right question."

Eric, down by the sea, walked and thought. After a while, he diverted into the town's worn-out shopping centre and sat at a tiled table, realising that, for the first time in as long as he could remember, he wasn't afraid of being seen in public. Though not naive enough to assume that everything from this point on was going to be alright, he nevertheless felt (having no more original description available) that a great weight had lifted from his shoulders.

When Carol finished her shift that afternoon, Eric took her for tea to the elegant Art-Deco hotel which dominated the promenade. Though recently restored, it was already faded by the needling salt.

On seeing the menu, she tried to protest – everything was so expensive – but he insisted that they needed to talk in a neutral environment. Last night, they'd dealt with history; today was for discussing what next.

"We could move back into the house up home," said Eric. "Start from there."

"No," said Carol. "Before anything, the police have to be told that you're alive. You can't go into the future with all these shadows hanging over. Whatever the consequences."

Eric, terrified and optimistic in equal measure, nodded but his inner doubts raged. The *You* and not *We*. She saw it on his face but knew the folly of settling for an easy solution. After tomorrow, she was on holiday until the day after Boxing Day.

After tomorrow, they would act.

## 65

It was Friday morning, the last before Christmas and Terry, in the hallway of the house, rang Penny Dalzell's secretary.

"You need to arrange an appointment through your GP," she told him.

"She said to call direct if I needed to see her urgently," said Terry.

"Is it urgent?"

"Well, I don't really know what…"

"Sorry. Mrs Dalzell's just walked in. I'll have a quick word."

Terry heard the curious echoing of a distant hand over a telephone mouthpiece backgrounded by quiet, unfathomable conversation. A shape appeared in the window of the front door and a cascade of envelopes sluiced through the letterbox onto the mat. Terry twisted around, trying to recognise handwriting or postmarks.

"Hello," said the uncovered voice.

"Yes?" said Terry, untwisting.

"It's Penny Dalzell. I'm on annual leave for two weeks from this afternoon."

"Oh, right," said Terry, and *at least I can tell Pat I tried*, he thought.

"But I can see you at 2.30 if that's any good?"

He decided to fill in the few hours until then by going into the office, even though he had plenty of work that could be done more efficiently at home. Eleanor in Reception seemed surprised to see him.

"Hello Terry," she said. "I thought you were sick."

"Only in my choice of reading materials," he said, then, "Who told you that?"

"Kate said you'd had a funny do yesterday."

"Well, I'm here."

He walked through the double doors into the corridor where his office was and saw Kate's door was open. He stopped and knocked. She looked up.

"Hello Kate. Eleanor says you've been telling people I had a funny do yesterday."

She turned bright red.

"I was just trying to…"

Her voice ground to a halt.

"I know," he said. "But don't."

Unlocking his own door, he spotted the Penguin Manager walking towards him, phone once again clenched to his face. Mistaking Terry's protracted stare for an attempt to begin a conversation, he shook his head sternly and pointed at his mobile with his free hand before raising the same hand, Cnut-like, to keep him at bayaway. In one crisp move, Terry swatted the phone to the floor and pretended to stamp on it. The other man looked terrified.

"You see," said Terry calmly, "if you mince around like that, making your dismissive gestures, you might upset people."

"I could have you sacked for this sort of behaviour," said Penguin.

"I doubt it. And in any case, to have me sacked, you'd have to know who I am."

The Dean, now uncertain, ducked down to retrieve the handset on the ground but Terry kicked it away.

"Fetch, Oswald," he said and went into his room.

A few minutes later, Wattabore from next door appeared.

"Hanniford just came in and asked me who you were. He said you'd attacked him."

"I didn't," said Terry. "Now, if you wouldn't mind, I've work to do. Merry Christmas, Howard."

He left at 1.45 for his appointment [meeting? what's the difference? there is one. or more] with Penny Dalzell. Locking his door, he wondered if it would be for the last time. It was a psychological motif for Terry, this contemplation of the ends of things.

Visiting his grandparents as a child, they would always send him home with a toy and, even then, he would be wondering how many toys there were to come before the ritual ended. This had nothing to do with a desire for acquisition, more of an anticipatory melancholy.

*All things must pass*, he thought, *which is why Hari Harrison ate so many prunes.*

His whole existence, capacity for pleasure, enjoyment, was compromised by the knowledge that everything would ultimately end. [*Which is sometimes a relief, as with this shitty job*]

En route to his appointment, he passed the pop-up gazebo of the local paper seller in the town centre. Today's billboard insert, pegged to a cute washing line stretched across the stall front, was unclear and indeterminate:

### MYSTERY OF DROWNING RESCUE HERO: LATEST

*Could the hero still be drowning*, he thought, *even as the papers flew off the pile?*

Terry, intrigued, abandoned his usual resistance, and bought a copy. On the front page was the headline,

### "I COULDN'T JUST LET HER DIE," SAYS LES

Two photos and an article sat underneath. One of the photos was the now-familiar farinaceous picture of Eric Bell, captioned with 'Modest Les leaves the hospital'; the second, a passport-like picture of, 'Les as he really looks'.

*What Les really looks*, thought Terry, *is NOTHING LIKE Eric Bell.*

The accompanying story, such as it was, cagily laid out the claim of local man, Les Jackson, that he'd been the hero who saved the girl. Short on detail and evidence to corroborate Les' assertion, Terry was impressed by the cynical, brazen publication of the story and wondered if tomorrow's probably already-planned exposure of Les Jackson as an opportunistic fantasist would shift as many papers as today's scoop.

When Terry went in to see Penny Dalzell [*on time, so definitely not a normal appointment*], she had the same colleague with her as on the first occasion: the one with the 'special interest' in him. This time, she introduced him.

"This is Sanjay Patel. He specialises in brain injury rehabilitation. We've been discussing your case."

[*It's not a case, it's a rucksack*]

"I don't have a brain injury," said Terry. "Nothing to rehabilitate."

"You present characteristics consistent with acquired brain injury," said Dr Patel. "Particularly regarding perceptions of reality, it seems."

"I think, therefore I am," said Terry unbidden, tears welling up. "Or am I?"

"Let's take it from there," said Dr Patel.

**66**

Eric Bell watched the birds hopping across the snow. An overnight fall had caught the salty air by surprise and the yard behind Carol's kitchen was thick with it.

Eric, to help the birds out in their winter struggles, had thrown eagerly-gobbled biscuits from the window. When the biscuits ran out, he discovered an out-of-date Christmas pudding at the back of a cupboard. That's when he realised he didn't know what to do with it, not because the birds wouldn't enjoy its sweet richness, but because he wasn't sure he was entitled to give it to them.

All through their married life, Eric and Carol had shared everything, without question. It had taken them a while to realise that their democratic approach to money and possessions was the exception rather than the rule amongst their friends and peers. In other relationships, it was common for one partner to assume control of the finances but this was never an issue with the Bells.

Now, in this unfamiliar yet half-filled with familiar things place, Eric doubted his right to decide the pudding's fate. Hand combing through hair, he was still anxiously mulling it over when Carol came in.

"Are you OK?" she said.

"The pudding. I wondered about giving it to the birds. Because it's your pudding."

"It's out of date and, anyway, if you're worried about who it belongs to, it's you that's the pudding."

"I wasn't sure. Didn't want to do the wrong thing."

She pulled his hand away from his head and squeezed it.

"Stop worrying about everything," she said. "It'll work out, you'll see."

"It will?" he said, trying not to sound doubtful.

"I'll have to go or I'll be late. I'll see you for the train at just after four. Make sure the front door's locked."

"OK," he said.

She kissed him on the forehead.

"Now, feed those birds."

Ernie was waiting for them on the cold platform when the train got in that night. Not given to being nervous, he was nevertheless unsure how Carol would react to the man who'd known all along that Eric was still alive but hadn't told her.

When they appeared at the top of the steps leading down from the footbridge, he had a dissilient sense of remorse at what he'd put her through. In the two years since he'd last seen her, Carol had aged ten. He wondered if the process was reversible. She caught sight of him and dropped Eric's arm.

"Hello Ernie," she said, offering him her handshake.

"Hello Carol," said Ernie, returning the gesture

There was a moment of uncertain silence then she pulled Ernie towards her and hugged him.

"It's good to see you again," she said.

Eric wiped his forehead in relief with his handkerchief and Ernie felt worse than ever.

The sweet smell of Camilla's cooking filled the air as they arrived at the house. She came into the hallway to greet them, no messing about with handshakes, straight into Carol's arms, a metaphysical '*too much time wasted already*' permeating the gathering.

When they'd eaten and cleared away, Camilla brought out the latest big weekly edition of the local paper. It contained a succinct bottom-of-the-front-page precis of the attempted drowning incident with more detailed coverage on Page 3.

"I've just got this," she said, spreading it on the table. "Thought I'd let you have first look at the hot story of the week."

As Terry anticipated, Les Jackson's hero claim had been rubbished and poor Les revealed as a serial fantasist now sentenced to ongoing trolling on social media. The little girl was safe and well with her grandma. Her mother, the thwarted killer, was in the care of local mental health services with whom she had a long and troubled history.

Eric, with typical reticence, had given Carol only a very brief and underplayed account of the events described and carefully watched as she read through the reports. Her face glowed with pride as she realised what her husband had done until she reached the final paragraph of the extended version. A sharp anxiety clouded her face and she looked up at the three faces watching her. She pointed at the paper and they crowded round to see what was wrong.

'Billy Rock', the girl's saviour had still not been identified but there was a worrying addition to the ongoing search for him in the form of a brief statement from Dr Sumaiya Khatun, the duty doctor who had seen him at the infirmary.

"Whilst I appreciate Mr Rock's desire to avoid publicity," she said, "on the basis of my examination of him after the incident, I urge him to contact the hospital as soon as possible."

# 67

Terry is resting at home. In his bed. In his head…

*Listen, the snow is falling.* [**Yoko is the Eggwoman.***]*

*Look up and the sky is kaleidoscoped by fluttering flakes over reddy blackground. My eyes are wet. Look down and the road is white. There is the street-light where we tied up Dennis Williamson. When his mother came out to take off the skipping-rope, we pelted her with marshmallows stolen from the back of the sweet factory. Then, the road was pink. The same road.*

*Between that light and the next, was Magic Lollipop Land. Believe in it and sweets would materialise on the hedges and bushes of the houses within its borders. Disbelieve and sweets were available at the little shop opposite the school where we found the injured bird lying in the doorway. The next day it was gone and the sweetshop owner said it had recovered and flown away but John Holmes said he didn't think it would have been able to fly because you twisted its head off, I saw you.*

*The same road where you could play because there weren't so many cars but still too many for Mary Thompson. She was there before cars, she said, and so was entitled to walk down the middle of the sweet-smelling tarmac, laid on the cheap, melting in the summer, trapping Mary Thompson in her plastic shoes so the steamroller could flatten her into the surface and no vehicle would ever again be held up.*

*Not the same road as the next road where Billy Graham (15), like Alice Cooper, a famous name but not the famous version, enticed us in to see his little sisters dancing naked, not exciting for anyone except him.*

*And the road after that where a bald-headed man with bulging eyes promised a meeting with the Northern Irish soccer team manager who'd be there at his house if we'd like to come along at 8pm next Tuesday night, no really he would, scouting for players, but we saw through him. Only Billy Graham kept the appointment.*

*The roads rose above the streets. You graduated upwards then you looked back down at where you'd come from. You looked down at the back lane where you, age six, rode the bike with your dad holding onto the saddle then you said Stop and you didn't because he'd let you go, you were on your own, then he remembered you didn't know what a brake was and ran after you, caught you but you were fired up, ready to do it again.*

*When Dad's lung collapsed and the sick pay ran out, Tommy Mills would come round with tins of food filched from the RAF base with the jets outside. He fixed planes and he rode bikes, Tommy Mills: loud-engined scramblers, deep-treaded, high wheels, spare framed, round muddy tracks until he had the heart attack cornering in the Sunday afternoon race at the airfield, only 37. No more tins. No more Tommy.*


*At school, playing the recorder. At Christmas, in assembly, Wee, three kings. [That's not funny.]*


### *BAGABCBABCBAGAFEE*


*the bridge between the chorus and the next verse. [Try it!] Clive Stubbs playing with his nose, dragged from the group and slippered before watching parents, that wouldn't happen now, everybody would sue everybody. Keep the fiscal dispersal in balance. Upside for Clive, he got his own recorder, not for him no more the grabbing from the germy red tray.*

*I thought this associative writing would be interesting, never-ending, would fill me with a glow. The glow of the sweet factory when it burned down. A street factory. Watching it from the roads above when we were 16, walking past the cemetery, seeing the thick smoke, the scent of cremated magic lollipops all around. Squeezing her hand.*

*But it wearies me. I can't clear the memory. The train robber on the loose, rumoured to be in our town, our district, our street, the thrill of running from shadows.*

*But it wearies me, the thinking. I'm not six or 11 or 16 anymore. I have the Lady of Shallot's view on shadows. I want some respite. I want to forget. I want the thinking to end.*

*For a while.*

Terry falls asleep.

# 68

# Is It a Criminal Offence to Go Missing?

Going *missing* is not an *offence*. Adults over the age of 18 have the right to *go missing* unless they have been detained under the Mental Health Act, or are legally in the care of another person. You will not be in any trouble for going *missing* unless you are wanted for a *crime*.

Eric Bell looked at the information on the website. The part about not being in any trouble made him wince. He had caused Carol terrible trouble, put her through emotional torture. Now, in retrospect, it seemed pointless. He had to keep in mind that he'd done it because he'd had her safety, her best interests, at heart. Changing circumstances mustn't be allowed to detract from his primary motivation. He had to remember this or he would go mad.

He felt he still hadn't fully explained his actions to her. Partly, this was because she wouldn't let him. After his initial description of events the day they met again, he had a curious feeling that she was keeping the conversation between them banal, mainly confined to the practical. If Eric attempted to go into deeper, more personal revelations, she would insist that the full facts would emerge in due course and there was no need for rushed, incomplete disclosures. The most important thing, she continued to emphasise, was that he was safe and well.

Eric, rather than being bolstered by her almost unquestioning acceptance of his sudden reappearance, felt irrationally anxious. In Carol's place, he knew he'd have been asking for a blow-by-blow account of the previous two years. He realised, on one level, that he should be grateful for her seeming sanguinity but it unnerved him.

The morning after their return, Eric, Carol and Camilla discussed what to do next. It was only three days until Christmas and Ernie, mindful of the importance of their customers' needs at this time of year, had already gone to open up the shop.

They made a short list:

1.  Tell the police about Eric's reappearance.
2.  Contact the insurance company about repaying the money given to Carol.
3.  Contact the cemetery to see about having Eric's gravestone removed.
4.  *Eric to get in touch with Sumaiya at the infirmary.*


Despite ostrich-like attempts at resistance from Eric, Carol and Camilla were insistent that the last item was the most important.

"I'd rather walk up there than ring them and get involved in a load of confusing discussions," he said at last.

"I'll tell Ernie to meet you," said Camilla. "Me and Carol will sort out the other matters."

Eric looked at his wife. She smiled reassuringly and he felt his love for her jolt through him like a bolt of forked lightning.

Burning rather than warming.

Walking openly to the hospital, Eric kept half-expecting to be recognised. It was a small town and he'd known a lot of people at one time or another. Today, though, the streets were quiet. The schools finished tomorrow and most Christmas shopping had been completed over the preceding weekend. It was, thought Eric, the calm before the inevitably dashed Yuletide expectations that characterised the festive season for him.

His ingrained pessimism stretched back across the years to that Christmas when his father, recently redundant from the printers he'd worked at since school, found stop-gap employment as a delivery driver. The day before Christmas Eve, he came home in the firm's little grey van and enlisted Eric and his long-gone sister to help unload the boxes from the back.

When they were all stacked up in the living-room, Eric's father had carefully opened each one and taken out the contents. Every box contained a different, expensive toy. There was a doll that cried when rocked, a clockwork train set, a small but sittable-on rocking horse and – the one Eric particularly loved – a big plastic wagon train with six horses and a giant set of Cowboys and Indians. Even now, Eric could remember the thrill of running the wagon train around the back kitchen, his father and sister in pursuit, howling as the Indians they were holding closed in on him.

Their playing went on for hours until, worn out, Eric and Margie went to bed exhausted and happy as he could ever remember.

The next morning, he rushed downstairs to continue the game and the toys were gone, now repacked and on their way to the homes of richer children north of the border. He was inconsolable.

Over the years, Eric had thought of this incident many times, acknowledging it as one of his life's defining experiences. The disappointment and sense of helplessness that had entered his being on that long-ago morning had never fully left him.

He reached the hospital reception desk and asked for Sumaiya. It transpired that she was a junior doctor and therefore of no fixed abode in the building, moving as she did between departments to gain experience. After making some phone calls, the receptionist located her supervisor and spoke to his secretary.

"Who should I say is here?" said the receptionist to Eric.

"Rock. Billy Rock," said Eric.

She gave him directions to the supervisor's office.

"I'm supposed to be meeting a friend here," said Eric in reply. "After I've seen the doctor."

He gave the woman a brief description of Ernie then went up to find Dr Khatun.

She was waiting outside the door when he arrived.

"Come in," she said, and ushered him inside. A man was sitting at the desk.

"Mr Rock, this is Mr Holgath," she said. "He's looking after me during my time here."

The man stood up and shook Eric's hand.

"Peter Holgath," he said.

"Eric Bell," said Eric. "It's a long story."

**69**

Terry had the letter from Penny Dalzell. He skimmed its contents. Sanjay Patel would begin treating him in January. They would see then if anything concrete materialised. Scans were clear. None of the psychometric tests they'd done was conclusive. Epilepsy remained a possibility. Even though he retained a high level of functionality when 'blanked out', he should avoid driving for now…

"What do you think?" he said to Pat.

"I think you may as well see him but don't expect too much. What do *you* think?"

"That I'm not too worried," he said. "That nobody knows what normal is anyway so I don't consider myself abnormal. I'm not dangerous or violent or aggressive or argumentative. I just have these episodes now when I didn't before. It's a question of modifying your sense of reality. There's people out there who *really* need help."

They went for a walk in the park. The snow from the South had arrived just too early for Christmas. As they wandered along arm-in-arm, Terry thought about his new reality. It was only the latest in an ongoing series. He would have to concentrate on his behaviour more but losing some of his inhibitions wasn't necessarily a bad thing. He had perhaps been too repressed before. So long as he didn't let his ego take him over…

*There were no answers to any of it. People seemed to have an innate desire for explanation and diagnosis, hence the infinity of attempts to impose order on a fundamentally chaotic world. He envied those with the ability [or was it a fortunate limitation of insight?] to sustain their denial, to lose themselves in shopping and fripperies and box-sets and drugs and all the rest of it.*

*And what of those whose denial broke down, whose illusions were ripped open? They populated the graveyards and the mental health facilities. Or they reinvented or ran away, or both. Or more? He wondered where Eric Bell was at this moment, not just physically but inside his own head. What had he been – was he going – through?*

    *The truth will out*, he thought.

    *Eventually.*

**70**

When Eric came back down into the hospital atrium, Ernie was waiting for him. They moved to sit at one of the tables belonging to the very expensive coffee franchise that had somehow gained purchase (and, doubtless, many *purchases)* in this prime selling spot. Ernie went to the counter. He came back and set down the tray.

"Lord, where is thy mercy?" he said. "There used to be a little hut thing downstairs. Run by a couple of old dears. You got a cup of cheap tea or shit instant coffee and a biscuit to take away the taste. When they built on this bit, the old dears got the boot and the corporates took over. Two lattes and you need a mortgage extension. This is a greedy country."

He looked at Eric but Eric wasn't really listening.

"What happened with the doctor?"

"She had another doctor with her. A cardiologist. They think there's something wrong with my heart. I've to have tests a s a p." Eric waved the appointment card in his hand. "After all that's gone on, just when things are getting back on track, this."

"That's one way of looking at it," said Ernie. "The other is to think that, if something does need fixing, you found out sooner rather than later. Saving the kid may prove to be a double victory in keeping you *both* alive."

Eric's fingers began tapping on the table and he was lost in his thoughts again. Ernie let him be and looked around.

At other tables, dressing-gowned patients sat with visiting relatives. Across the hallway, people waited outside this morning's clinics, not yet knowing what news they'd be taking home later. Lifts from the wards upstairs clattered open and blue-clad orderlies pushed out trolleys that contained either supplies or patients bound for who knows where. Through the misted-up glass panels at the entrance, Ernie saw yet more patients huddled outside on the snow-covered pavement smoking enthusiastically, the very cause of why some of them were here providing the only effective palliative for their anxieties.

Eric, his bladder squeezed by nerves, went off to the toilet whilst Ernie cleared the cups away and rang Camilla.

"Cam, Eric's done and we're walking home. I managed to get Janice in to do the shop till two."

"How is he?" she said.

"OK. He saw some heart doctor. They're going to do tests. Good rather than ominous ones, I'd imagine. Is Carol OK?"

Camilla's voice dropped conspiratorially.

"Tell you later. She's on the phone to the insurance company at the minute. Opening line of 'Let's Face The Music And Dance'."

"Crikey," said Ernie.

"Yes," said Camilla.

Eric returned relieved and the two men exited into the crisp morning. Christmas music coming from the hospital's residential ward to their right was dopplered out as an emergency ambulance flew up the driveway heading for A&E but, this short intrusion aside, the day had a calm quietness to it.

Today's local paper billboard outside the first newsagent on the main road announced a 'Free Chocolate Tree Decoration For Every Reader.' Real news had been temporarily suspended.

"How about we go in, buy a paper and say 20 people in our house are gonna read it?" said Ernie. "Do you think he'll give us 20 chocolate reindeer?"

"Give it a try," said Eric distractedly.

"Eric. Are you alright?"

"Not really," said Eric. "I think I've left things too late."

"No, you'll be OK. If the heart thing was really serious, they'd have kept you in today."

"Not that," said Eric. "Carol."

# 71

Across the fabric of the town, disparate threads of Eric Bell and Terry Ellis's present, past and tangential lives wove on in oblivious isolation.

Somewhere out there [*isn't that the title of a terrible by-numbers song from some mawkish movie?*], Julie Diggle giggled as her brother didn't see the hole beneath the snow and couldn't get her wheelchair (and her) back out and onto the path.

Ken McKie and the other three staff in the Bereavements office had mince pies with their lunch and one had something hard in it that cracked Melanie's tooth.

Mr Nuttall, long-ago Head of Lower School, was waiting with his young Filipino wife for the airport coach, both happy and looking forward to two weeks in the South European sun.

Terry saviours, Phil and Helen with baby Lizzie were expecting Helen's parents at any minute from Blackpool for a mixed-feelings-on-both-sides week together.

The Richardson family was awaiting the outcome of young Danny's first court appearance and neither knew of nor cared about recently-deceased, generally reviled but possibly very well-off Uncle Lewis's old grudges.

Teresa Green was lost in the Lunchtime Special show at the cinema, watching the digitally-restored version of *Goldfinger*, free custard creams balanced on a paper plate on her seat arm.

Bad-Knees Bob's friend, Geordie had had his test results and all was unexpectedly well so Bob was buying him a celebratory lunch.

Life, like Ole Man River, just kept rolling along.

# 72

And Eric Bell? Eric Bell was right. Possibly.

"I only met him a month ago," said Carol.

"You'd already seen me by then," said Eric. "On the platform. You knew I was still alive."

"Yes," said Carol, "but I didn't know if *I* was."

"And are you?" said Eric.

"I'm not sure yet," said Carol.

"When you find out," said Eric Bell, "let me know."